DRIVE EAST ON 66

Police Lieutenant Andy Bastian is hired to drive young teenager Ralph Bartlett from California to Kansas, traveling east on Route 66. Ralph's rich father has booked his brilliant but unstable son into a mental clinic for treatment, and wants the arrangement to be kept secret from the public. Accompanying them is Olga Beaumont, a psychiatrist who has been hired to care for Ralph. But before they've gone far, Andy realizes they're being followed. Then they discover that their car's been sabotaged, and narrowly escape death . . .

SPECIAL MESSAGE TO READERS

**THE ULVERSCROFT FOUNDATION
(registered UK charity number 264873)**

was established in 1972 to provide funds for
research, diagnosis and treatment of eye diseases.
Examples of major projects funded by
the Ulverscroft Foundation are:-

- The Children's Eye Unit at Moorfields Eye
  Hospital, London
- The Ulverscroft Children's Eye Unit at Great
  Ormond Street Hospital for Sick Children
- Funding research into eye diseases and
  treatment at the Department of Ophthalmology,
  University of Leicester
- The Ulverscroft Vision Research Group,
  Institute of Child Health
- Twin operating theatres at the Western
  Ophthalmic Hospital, London
- The Chair of Ophthalmology at the Royal
  Australian College of Ophthalmologists

You can help further the work of the Foundation
by making a donation or leaving a legacy.
Every contribution is gratefully received. If you
would like to help support the Foundation or
require further information, please contact:

**THE ULVERSCROFT FOUNDATION
The Green, Bradgate Road, Anstey
Leicester LE7 7FU, England
Tel: (0116) 236 4325
website: www.foundation.ulverscroft.com**

RICHARD WORMSER

◆

DRIVE EAST ON 66

Complete and Unabridged

LINFORD
Leicester

First published in Great Britain

First Linford Edition
published 2018

A catalogue record for this book is available
from the British Library.

ISBN 978–1–4448–3890–9

Published by
F. A. Thorpe (Publishing)
Anstey, Leicestershire

Set by Words & Graphics Ltd.
Anstey, Leicestershire
Printed and bound in Great Britain by
T. J. International Ltd., Padstow, Cornwall

This book is printed on acid-free paper

1

In our town of five thousand houses, the Bartlett house was the largest. This was no accident; Sidney Bartlett had planned it that way when he built the other four thousand, nine hundred and ninety-nine homes; your choice of ranch, split-level or traditional, two bedrooms or three, no down payment, GI, low move-in cost, FHA.

Our town, I suppose, is far from unique; there are a dozen more like it in southern California, and I hear that you can find its twin in the San Francisco area, around New York, Boston, Philadelphia, a dozen other cities.

They weren't here twenty years ago, and sometimes I get the feeling that they won't be here twenty years from now. But in the meantime, Mr. Bartlett was rolling in money, honestly earned; the five thousand construction jobs had been solid, workmanlike and in all respects up to standard, GI or FHA.

I had only been in the Bartlett house once before, in the year I'd lived in Naranjo Vista, which was what our town was called. There was no swank about Sidney Bartlett; if he had a butler, or even a maid, he still answered the door himself. He shook my hand, called me Lieutenant Bastian before I had a chance to identify myself, and pulled me in with a hand on my sleeve. 'Put your cap there, and come into my study. We'll have a drink and break the ice.'

I said: 'I'm sorry, Mr. Bartlett, I don't drink in uniform.'

He said: 'Then take your coat off. Or jacket, or tunic, or whatever you call it.'

'It's not that, sir.' I grinned, aware that I sounded stuffy. 'But the way people drive, I could have a bump-up on my way home. I'd show lousy with liquor on my breath and a police uniform on my back.'

Mr. Sidney Bartlett frowned. I suppose he wasn't used to getting anything but his own way, especially in the town he'd built and chosen to live in. He said: 'You didn't have to wear your uniform. You do drink, don't you?'

2

'Sure,' I said. 'I'm sorry if I sound a prig.' I watched, and his eyebrows shifted a little, I hoped in surprise that I knew words like that. 'I smoke and drink and chase women.'

'Then that decides it. You'll have the drink. Take a chair.' He smiled, though the deeply grooved frown didn't go away. 'I'm sorry to make such a big issue of such a little thing, but the truth is, there's some ice needs breaking. We're going to have to talk pretty frankly, get to know each other very well very quickly, and a drink — ' He threw his hands up in a gesture that was almost French; a strange movement in a man who could have been a rancher or a western banker or a shopkeeper, but certainly not a Parisian. My face doesn't show anything unless I want it to; I didn't want it to just then.

We went through a glassed in-hall showing a dining room on one side and a huge beamed living room on the other; the living room was lined with books and paintings, and there was an Oriental rug on the floor that even I knew ought to be in a museum.

He opened a door into a much smaller room that had almost as many books in it. The rug here was Navajo, though, brown and yellow and black and white. I had to step on it, and I sank in a little; I've never seen an Indian rug woven that thick.

Mr. Bartlett said: 'Finian, this is Lieutenant Bastian,' very gravely, and a tiny gray dog jumped out of a leather chair and stretched as though he were bowing to me. I reached down, and he let me pat him, and then curled up in the exact middle of the Navajo.

'He's a Yorkshire terrier,' my host said. 'They don't shed. Take his chair; you won't get hair on your uniform. Bourbon and soda all right?'

'Fine,' I said. 'And I don't take the uniform quite that seriously.'

Sidney Bartlett had opened a walnut cabinet and was pouring bourbon into monogrammed glasses. The quiet label on the bottle said it was eight years old; ads I had read had said it was the most expensive bonded bourbon on the market.

If you make a hundred dollars apiece on five thousand houses, you have made a half million dollars. And Naranjo Vista was not the only town he had built.

I said: 'You sent me a bottle of that whiskey for Christmas.'

He nodded. 'I wanted to give you something much more expensive, but the chief said no.'

'The old army rule,' I said. 'Don't accept any gifts you can't use up in a week.'

He handed me my drink and sat down in the swivel chair behind the walnut desk. The little dog raised one eyelid at him and then went back to sleep. Sidney Bartlett didn't bother with a toast, which pleased me. He said: 'That's right, you're an old army man. On pension, aren't you?'

'Half pay,' I said. 'Twenty years active duty; from seventeen to thirty-seven.'

'Your whole life.' He gave that shrug again. 'And then you change army OD for police blue. I can see why you're uniform-conscious.'

'I wish we'd never gotten on the subject of uniforms,' I said. 'But as long as we did, I've worn one since I can remember.

It was an orphanage uniform before I got old enough to enlist.'

He took a deep drag on his highball and exhaled. He muttered something, but not loud enough for me to be sure what it was. Whatever it was, he sounded sad enough. He snapped his fingers, and the little terrier woke up, looked around, and then came and jumped in my lap. 'Getting old,' Bartlett said. 'He gets confused. I call him to be petted, and he goes to you. In another fifteen or twenty years, maybe you'll sympathize with him . . . I'm pretty old myself.'

I let him make what he wanted to out of watching me work on my drink.

He said: 'We might as well start. In the first place, I've cleared this with your chief. I don't mean I've told him what I want you to do; just that I want your services for two weeks, on a personal matter. He said it was fine with him, but that he couldn't guarantee you'd do it; that you were your own man.' He stopped, hauled an old-fashioned gold watch out of the top of his pants, and looked at it. I ran my fingers through the little dog's hair and waited. I am very good at waiting.

'I've got two other men coming to talk with us,' Mr. Bartlett said. 'My lawyer and the family doctor . . . There's nothing illegal about this, not at all. Nor dangerous to you. And the job pays a thousand dollars, and shouldn't take you the full two weeks. I don't see what would keep you from accepting it.'

It was time for me to talk. I said: 'You haven't told me what it is you want me to do,' and sat tense, waiting to hear. A thousand dollars is a lot of money, to me at least.

But instead of just laying the job out, he had to do some more bush-beating. 'I liked what you did last year, Lieutenant Bastian. I don't mean that you kept my house from being robbed; naturally I liked that. But that you took the burglar without hurting him. You'd have been within your rights if you'd shot him to death.'

'We aren't trained that way in the MPs.'

'I suppose not. Your drink holding out all right? I see that it is . . . This is very

7

hard, Lieutenant.'

Now he had run down completely and slumped into his chair, staring at his half-drunk drink. I said: 'My first name's Andrew, Mr. Bartlett.'

'Andy,' he said. 'I'm almost old enough to be your father.'

'Not unless *your* father was a maharajah,' I said. But he didn't smile; instead he gulped the rest of the drink and went back to staring at the empty glass. I got up and took it away from him, and made him another highball.

He said: 'Thanks. I — ' He shook his head, and I could have sworn he was about to cry. But he drank instead, and seemed to get courage.

'Yesterday,' he said. 'Yesterday, my son . . . All you have to do for me, Andy, is take my son for a ride.' He thought how that sounded, and rephrased. 'For a drive. Drive east on Highway 66. A thousand miles, give or take a hundred. It's nothing.'

'Nothing,' I said. 'Fifty dollars and a little expense money. Gas, meals, a couple of motel rooms. Two days each way

. . . I've got a fairly good car.'

'Take mine,' he said absently. 'There isn't anybody doesn't enjoy driving a Cadillac convertible that's almost new.' He looked at me and he tried to smile, and I sat as still as I know how, waiting for the gimmick, the hook. This was not just a way of trying to pay me back for catching a burglar for him. That had been part of my job as night lieutenant of his police force.

Because he paid us, the police department were employees of his. The sheriff had to approve of each of us, but the Bartlett Construction Company paid us; it was part of the deal on the five thousand houses — police and fire protection free for ten years. He didn't owe me a thing.

He said: 'I told you, my doctor and my lawyer will be here any moment. Which should assure you that there's nothing illegal about to happen, to be mentioned . . . So — it's not hard to read your mind, because it's what I'd be thinking — what am I about to pay you for?'

Back when I was still a sergeant in the

army, we had a company commander who rated his MPs on how good they were at shooting rabbits. In your spare time, you had to take a .22 out in the woods and pot at bunnies. That was how I got to go to OCS: shooting rabbits. I didn't like rabbit meat, and I got no strange sexual thrill out of watching long-eared death throes, but I learned, move at the wrong time, and your bunny gets away.

This rabbit was worth a thousand dollars. I sat still.

'You don't help me much,' Mr. Bartlett said. He turned the glass in his fingers. 'All right. I'm paying you for keeping your mouth shut. Before you go, and when you come back. I don't want your chief to know about this, or any of the other police officers, or your wife, if you ever marry.'

The time had come to talk a little. 'Mr. Bartlett, I'm not about to marry. But so far as the chief goes — he's a smart cookie, sir. A sharp policeman. There isn't much in this town that happens that he doesn't know about sooner or later. If he finds out about this, whatever it is, I don't want you blaming me.'

He nodded and stood up. His glass was empty; he took a couple of steps towards the liquor cabinet, then stopped, shook his head decisively, and set the glass down on his desk hard. 'There's no answer in a bottle,' he said. 'Help yourself if you want to. No . . . ? I'll take my chances on you, Andy. I mean on not talking. I — ' Then, suddenly, he laughed. 'Cops. Pride yourselves on being in the know, don't you? Something you and your chief don't know. My son's crazy,' he said. 'I want you to drive him to an insane asylum.'

There was enough shock in the words to make me forget my careful self. 'People don't talk that way. Not anymore. Your son has a bad neurosis. I'm to take him to a sanitarium for treatment.'

Then, for a moment, we weren't a man who wanted a thousand dollars and another man who wanted to buy discretion for a shameful secret. We were just two guys. He said: 'What do you mean, not anymore?'

'Not up here with the big money and the wide streets. That's talk from back in the orphanage and the GI bar racks.'

One of us probably got control back before the other. I sat back in my chair, and he went around behind the desk and was the executive in the swivel seat, tilting his fingertips together. His voice could have been asking me to bid on wiring a hundred houses, or supplying sand for the cement mixers on a job. 'If he tries to get away from you, you're the officer who took that burglar without — without violence. Take him back the same way.'

I was full of questions, like, was the boy curable? Like, did we have to tell him where he was going? Like — I wasn't to get a thousand dollars for asking what wasn't my business. I said: 'I'm a police officer, not a doctor. If he has an attack or whatever on the way, what do I do?'

'A young woman goes with you,' Mr. Bartlett said. 'A graduate student in psychology from the university.'

Faintly, a bell tinkled. 'The front door,' Mr. Bartlett said. 'The doctor or the lawyer. You'll want to talk to them?'

'If they want to,' I said. 'I'd rather meet the boy.'

2

Mr. Bartlett and a man who he said was Dr. Martin stood near the front door and watched while I rapped on the handsome limed oak they said led to the boy's apartment, his wing of the big new house. Ralph, they said the boy's name was. Ralphie.

A key worked on the other side of the door. It opened; a young woman stood there. Tall, about five seven or eight, and thin.

'I'm Andy Bastian,' I said. 'I'm going to drive Ralph to Kansas.'

The eyes were gray, with just a touch of blue. They closed, and then opened again, saying yes, she knew. 'Come on in. Ralph's reading. I'm Olga Beaumont.'

'And how is Fletcher these days?'

She failed to be impressed. 'Dead, I presume, since Beaumont and Fletcher were contemporaries of William Shakespeare.'

13

'Ouch. I was just trying to prove I'd read a book.'

'Don't bother. I don't like policemen. I don't mean I dislike you; I don't know you. But I dislike the idea of the police. I think there must be a weakness in any man who takes up law enforcement for a life's work.'

My head was shaking all by itself. I had always heard that screw-tighteners and people who worked in sanitariums got a little odd themselves. Now it seemed to be proving out. I thought of rapping her with a brisk line of police talk, starting with 'Sister — ' and then let it go. 'I came here to talk to Ralph.'

'He's reading. He doesn't like to be interrupted.'

'Does he get violent?'

The gray eyes stared at me. Then the blue in them was more apparent. 'No, not really, whatever you've heard. He's disturbed, there's no doubt about it, but — ' She stopped. 'Anyway, you're a big strong man, and he's a little boy. You don't have to be afraid.'

'Don't carry your cop-hating far

enough to make your back ache. I'm leaving my badge here.'

She sighed and walked ahead of me down a short hall. There were two places on the wall, rectangles that showed lighter than the rest of the paint; pictures had hung there recently. Without knocking, she opened a door.

Ralph was a little boy, she'd said, but the legs that sprawled around the heavy white leather chair were longer than mine; he'd be taller than me when he stood up, but he'd weigh fifty pounds less, and I am not a fat man.

His hair was mussed, and getting no better from the beating he was giving it with his right hand. The left was helping his knee hold up a heavy red cloth book. First the left knee would push the book up towards his glasses, then the right. He was an expert squirmer.

Miss Beaumont said his name; she got less response than I'd earned with my crack about Beaumont and Fletcher. She cleared her throat and said: 'Lieutenant Bastian's going to drive us to Kansas.'

This did it. The bony fingers tore out a

small lock of hair, put it in the book for a place mark, and closed the book carefully. Light-colored eyes blinked, refocusing themselves, and Ralph said: 'What kind of a lieutenant?'

I looked around the room; up till now I'd been concentrating on him. One side of it was book-lined, like his father's study, though with harder-used books. Then there was the big leather chair — again, like his father's, but white instead of tan — and that was it. There wasn't even a carpet on the hardwood floor.

Miss Beaumont made some kind of a noise in her throat and went away.

Ralph said: 'I tore up all the furniture yesterday, but you can sit here if you want.' He showed as much regret as a soda jerk announcing he'd sold all the raspberry ice.

'No, thanks. A policeman gets used to leaning on walls.'

Ralph slung his improbable legs over the arm of the chair. 'Oh, you're that kind of lieutenant. Tell me, are you experimental, or intuitive?'

The noise I made was no more intelligible than Miss Beaumont's had been.

Ralph laughed. 'What I mean is this. Say you are given a crime to solve. There are two ways of going about it: the empirical, or trial-and-error approach, would be to accuse everyone possible of the crime, one at a time, and thus to find the suspect the circumstances fit, and convict her or him. The intuitive or abstract inference way would be to sit perfectly still, thinking, until you have eliminated all but one suspect.'

I scratched my shoulders against the wall and shoved my hands deep in my pants pockets. One of the windows was starred, no doubt from Ralph's furniture destruction. I said: 'Well, we use a combination of both. Of course, a man likes to use his brain. But the taxpayers expect him to use his feet.'

Ralph nodded. He groped around in the inside pocket of his rumpled coat and got out a silver pencil and a little leather notebook, and made a note of my deathless words. 'In this town, my father's the only taxpayer.'

'Yes. For the first ten years, anyway.'

'Of course, that isn't really so. The price of police and fire protection, sewer and street maintenance and so on was added onto the price of the houses. Actually, taking the average cost of such services in cities of this size in the United States, Father can pay for everything out of the interest — at six and a half per cent — on that extra charge. Since this is southern California, and equipment — cars, street sweepers, fire trucks — last much longer where there isn't any snow, I suspect that it wouldn't be more than six percent, though I haven't worked that out yet . . . When are we leaving for Kansas?'

'Tomorrow morning, early. Okay with you?'

'Oh, yes. I'm anxious to get to the clinic. I suspect I'll pick up a good deal on abnormal psychology there. We can have some good talks about criminology on the way.'

'I ought to be able to learn a lot in a thousand miles.'

'Yes,' Ralph said. 'Really, though, Miss Beaumont could have driven me. My violent periods are quite rare.'

I waved a feeble hand and got out of there. He had already opened the book by the time I got my hand on the doorknob. The book-marking hair floated to the bare floor.

Miss Beaumont was waiting in the hall, not leaning on anything.

'I'm turning the duty back to you,' I said.

She smiled, slightly. It changed her face completely; there was nothing cold about her smile at all. 'Ralph give you a hard time?'

'If I had a dog, and he suddenly started talking like Einstein, I'd be more surprised. But I don't have a dog.'

She didn't smile. 'I hope you do have a cigarette. I've been out all day.'

I fished out a package, and she opened one of the doors and waved for me to go in. Her room, apparently, because a closet door was slightly open, and I could see women's clothes inside. Not women's — woman's. Bright stuff, a silly hat on a shelf, a sweater with a silly bear embroidered on the front. I held a match for her, but I kept on looking into the closet. High-heeled shoes, very spiky, on the floor. I looked down at the sensible flats on her feet.

She flushed and got up and closed the closet door. 'I suppose a detective is a detective all the time.'

But I had taped her now. I said: 'You're very afraid of losing this job, aren't you? Of having Mr. Bartlett think you're too young or too frivolous for it?'

She studied me for a moment and then, unexpectedly, broke into a real grin. 'Okay,' she said. 'You win, detective. Getting a Ph.D. in psychology's expensive, and if there are any rich Beaumonts, we're not part of them.'

'I suppose Fletcher got all the royalties.'

She laughed. 'I ought to say that a little learning is a dangerous thing, but you might pull out your blackjack and conk me . . . It's good to see a strange face in this house, and yours is kind of strange. Do you arrest criminals by hitting them with your nose?'

Now she had me laughing, too. She stopped it by saying: 'In front of Ralph,

I'm very cold, very proper. Anything else scares him.'

'Should he be left alone?'

She stopped smiling and puffed on her cigarette greedily, as though she couldn't afford smoking very often. 'He's absorbed in that book. And the truth is, he's harmless.'

'Harmless. He bragged about breaking up all the furniture yesterday.'

'*And* a window,' Miss Beaumont said. 'But not his books. And not the chair he likes to read in. His father can buy more furniture, but some of the books are pretty rare.'

'Oh.' Then I had to add something. 'Where were you when all this was going on?'

'In the big white chair,' Miss Beaumont said. 'It seemed a good chance to test his hostility towards me, or the lack of it. He threw a number of things at me, but they all missed.'

This was a woman who believed in giving her all for science. I bit the inside of my cheek, because if I grinned now, she might start throwing things, and I doubted if she'd miss. I let her know that the police department was not entirely devoid of brains. 'He's hostile to women,' I said.

For the first time since the grin, she looked at me as though I was something more than a piece of furniture too big to throw. 'How did you guess that, Lieutenant Bastian?'

'Just call me Andy,' I said. 'Handy Andy, the chauffeur. Why, our boy gave me a short talk on crime detection. He said: 'convict her or him' instead of 'him or her, as the case may be,' which was what I'd expect him to say.'

Miss Beaumont nodded. 'Very good,' she said, just like my arithmetic teacher back in the fourth grade. 'I'm very careful to wear extremely plain tailored clothes, and this is hardly the hairdo I'd pick for myself.'

Well, three good brains were going east to Kansas together. Two sets rated at maybe one and a quarter each, and one halfwit makes three. That fourth-grade arithmetic comes in handy now and then. 'I'd better get back to Mr. Bartlett. Eight in the morning too early for you?'

'Fine.'

'How about Bartlett?' I asked. 'Divorced, widowed?'

Miss Beaumont said: 'When he hired me, he said he was a widower.'

'Volunteered it?'

The woman said: 'It came out curiously. He asked me if I wanted another woman to stay here with me. In this day and age I didn't know what he meant; and then he explained that, though a widower, I was quite safe alone in the house with him. I almost laughed.'

'That's something I'll bet you don't do enough of, and I don't mean almost.' I left her with that, and went back to the main wing. But not until she'd unlocked the door that cut off Master Ralph's wing of the house. Ralph might not be violent, but she was being conscientious. I caught myself wondering what she'd look like in fancier clothes, fluffier hair, the spike heels I'd seen in her closet.

A black man in a white coat was just carrying an empty tray out of Mr. Bartlett's study. He held the door for me, and I went in. Mr. Bartlett and Dr. Martin and a man called Mr. Nehemoff — the lawyer, no doubt — all had highballs in their hands. I declined one, and took the fourth leather chair.

Mr. Nehemoff said: 'Well, Lieutenant?'

'Well enough,' I said. 'Ralph's agreed to start at eight tomorrow morning. He seems anxious to get it over with.'

The lawyer sighed. 'Then I won't bother talking to him.'

'You should. He'd probably clear you up on some of the differences between *corpus delicti* and *res gestae*.'

Mr. Nehemoff grunted. 'Not that I couldn't use it.'

Dr. Martin said: 'He's an extraordinary boy. While I was wait — while I was with him yesterday, he gave me a summation of the various studies on virus mutation made in the past few years. I must say, like you, Nehemoff, I could use it. Stuff there I'd been meaning to read up on for months. He's a very bright lad, Sidney.'

Mr. Bartlett said: 'Cold comfort, Joe.'

The doctor shrugged. 'People with his intelligence are liable to go off now and then. They see more than the rest of us, feel it more, I suppose. I don't know; I'm an internist, not a psychiatrist, thank God. But the clinic will let you know. They're supposed to be the best in the world, in their specialty.' He sounded as though any MD who specialized in psychiatry was probably a pervert.

I said: 'Well, I've got packing to do, and so on. Anything I need to know about my legal status, Mr. Nehemoff?'

The lawyer said: 'No. You're *in loco parentis*, since you started bringing Latin in. Ralph's under age, sixteen to be exact, and his father has delegated you to take him to these doctors in Kansas. In other words, you have all the rights of a father while en route. They're practically unlimited.'

'Okay. Dr. Martin, how about drugs, if necessary? Sedatives? Narcotics?'

Dr. Martin looked up at the ceiling. 'Ralph himself has some tranquilizers, if he feels the need for them.'

I shook my head. 'Yesterday he broke up a pile of furniture — though Mr. Bartlett assured me he wouldn't be violent. You drugged him then . . . ' I flapped my big hand at the doctor before he could tell a lie and have to have his mouth washed out. 'You started to say you were waiting with him yesterday, then changed it to plain with him. You were waiting for him to pass out, weren't you?'

Dr. Martin said: 'He's an awfully good boy. I'll send over a couple of Syrettes of morphine to put your mind at rest. Okay?'

'Okay,' I said. 'I'll see myself out, Mr. Bartlett. And I can drive myself home; it's been an hour since I had that highball. I'll leave my car here tomorrow.' I started for the door, then turned and faced them. 'I don't exactly get it,' I said. 'Three people — a doctor, a psychologist and you, Mr. Bartlett — have assured me Ralph isn't violent. But yesterday he did a house-wrecking job a wild elephant would have been proud of.'

They gave me three sets of middle-aged stares. Finally Nehemoff dropped his eyes, but the other two outstared me.

'Okay,' I said. 'I hope you know what

you're doing. If anybody has any idea of playing me for some kind of a patsy, those things backfire.'

3

In the morning I parked my car under the Bartlett carport, between a Cadillac convertible and an Ambassador station wagon. I heaved my overnight bag into the convertible, since Mr. Bartlett had mentioned that car, and got my tool kit out of the turtle deck of my own heap, and did what needed to be done. I was just finishing up when the house help came out, carrying two boxes — books, from the way he strained with them. He set them down and opened the trunk of the Cad, and I helped him load them. He went around and got my bag from the seat, and put that in, too. 'Just a suitcase for Ralph and a little bag like yours for Miss Beaumont to come,' he said. 'Plenty of room. Want me to put in a bottle or so of drinking whiskey, Lieutenant? They tell me Kansas is dry.'

'Not any more. There's several states between here and there, and I don't drink

28

much,' I said. 'So, no thanks.'

He grinned without meaning, and then went around to see what I'd been doing with my tools. He nodded. 'Yes,' he said. 'I see. But you don't have to worry.'

'Ralph isn't violent,' I said.

'That's right. One of the nicest boys I ever knew. A real head! If this country had a hundred like Ralph, but grown up, we wouldn't have to worry about Russia.'

'There's a thought.'

'Want some breakfast, Lieutenant? Miss Beaumont and Ralph are eating theirs.'

'I'm shaved, bathed and fed. I'll wait for them in the car. By the way, here are the keys to mine. You might want to use it while I'm gone.'

He said that it was very thoughtful of me to think of that, took the keys, and went into the house. When he came out again, I was behind the wheel. I stayed there while he put the rest of the luggage in the car and slammed the trunk lid. Then he came around and handed me a small package.

'From Mr. Bartlett. He said to tell you

it's medicine from the doctor and expense money from him. And good luck, Mr. Bartlett said.'

'Where is he, this fine California morning?' A fog was drifting around, smelling of orange groves and the artificial rubber factories all at once.

'Still in bed. Or in his room, at least. He rings for me when he wants his coffee, before he shaves.' His face was shiny with effort. 'They're not going to hurt Ralph at this place where he's going, are they?'

That needed some thinking over. I puffed my cigarette, and then threw it away and said: 'Probably no worse than not having his father come and say goodbye. But I don't know. We're hired hands, you and I. His father and the doctor and the lawyer say he ought to go there; so I take him. Where's his mother?'

Brown eyes stared at me. 'Why, dead, I always thought. Isn't she, Lieutenant?'

'I wouldn't have asked if I knew.'

My voice must have barked. His face changed. I was a cop and he was a servant. He said: 'Yes, sir,' and turned away.

Too bad, I thought. Too bad. You become an expert in a number of things in twenty-one years of copping — traffic control, criminal investigation, how to break up a mob, how to run a jail or patrol on foot or in a car. But you forget how to be a friend. You don't have to be friendly; your badge insures respect. Too bad. That was a nice guy, and for a few minutes he had levelled with me, man to man. I lit another cigarette. The fog was breaking up, turning from blue to yellow as the sun bit through it. My watch said five minutes to eight.

Mr. Bartlett had built his house on a little knoll, one of the few elevations in Naranjo Vista. A street led up to it, curving as all the streets did, and then widened into a turn around, with riot fencing to keep kids from driving out into the fields to neck.

The fields where the vista stopped were planted to poinsettias. Some Japanese were out there, stooping along, working as though they'd been there since midnight, and would be there till midnight tonight. I wondered what they

31

thought, looking over at the town, at Mr. Bartlett's beautiful house. Probably nothing except that they'd gotten the rent of the fields cheap, for agreeing to plant flowers. There had been dairy farms there before Mr. Bartlett started to develop the Vista . . .

The door of the house opened, and Miss Beaumont came out. She was dressed in a tan gabardine suit that was almost O.D., a high-necked white blouse with a gold pin ornamenting the V. She had an over-the-shoulder bag, not so big as a WAC's, and a big tan beret. Neat, but far, far from gaudy.

She walked to the car without looking back, and behind her Ralph stopped and shook hands with the house-man. A white-coated arm suddenly shot around Ralph's shoulders, and gave him a brotherly hug; the servant had to reach up to do it, as Ralph was a head taller than the man.

I got out of the car and went around and opened the door for Miss Beaumont. She asked me where I wanted her to sit.

'The middle,' I said. 'A lady between

two gents. Any other arrangement would be too clinical.' I grinned into her cold stare, and kept on grinning until she showed through the psychologist's bland face for a moment, and she smiled. 'A thousand miles ahead,' I said. 'Take it easy, and we'll make it, a mile at a time.'

A car came down the block, a maroon two-door small Buick, two years old, two men in it. A mistake, apparently, because it went into the turn around, braking too fast, and then went back up the street again.

The last puffs of fog rolled towards us, and Miss Beaumont reached over to shut the right-hand door. But Ralph was there. He slid in and slammed the door after him. 'Hope I didn't keep you waiting, Lieutenant?'

'Right on the button of eight,' I said. 'Or thereabouts.' I started the motor, slid the shift into drive, and we rolled.

'Just a minute,' Ralph said. 'Something I forgot.'

I stopped the car, and he reached down for the door handle, and then saw there wasn't any. He said: 'Oh.'

I started to get out to let him out, but he said: 'It doesn't matter. It was my microscope, but they're sure to have one at a hospital, aren't they?'

'Sure to,' Miss Beaumont said. 'A better one than yours. In fact, I haven't seen one like yours since I took general science in high school.'

We were moving again; out of the driveway down the street, through the Vista. A patrol car passed us, moving slowly, making the morning check on parked cars. A sergeant, Nat Driscoll, was driving. Before I thought, I honked softly at him twice, and he honked back.

Ralph said: 'I'd like to see the world through a policeman's eyes once. Where we see a bush, he sees a possible traffic hazard; where we see a new car, he sees a license plate that might be stolen; where we see a nice view, what does he see? A place for a murder, a rendezvous for kidnappers? It would be interesting.'

Here we go. A thousand miles of this. I said: 'You know, we use microscopes in police work.'

Ralph was very polite. 'I know.

Comparative ballistics. It's merely a convenience; a good magnifying glass would be all you need.' We had gotten rid of the Vista and were going up the ramp of the freeway. He looked at the planting that kept the dirt walls from falling down into the roadway and said: 'I wonder how ice plant got its name. It's an import from the Mediterranean basin, you know.'

I hadn't known. He went on like that. The passing of a foreign car led him to make a speech on the difficulties of making a V-six engine; this naturally brought him to the V-12 or Lincoln Continental, its history, the faults in its design, its virtues, and its lack of resemblance to the Continental Mark II. Mention of the Mark II reminded him of World War I ammunition, since they had used a fuse called the Mark II in shrapnel. He didn't approve of shrapnel. He said — he said a lot of things.

We were moving along in the torrent of freeway traffic. The Cadillac was beauti-fully balanced, and full of oomph and ambition. The only thing that passed us was a slew of Volkswagens, like fleas swimming ahead of a fox with a stick in his mouth, if that story is true.

I was tempted to ask Ralph if foxes really got rid of fleas by swimming upstream with a stick, when Miss Beaumont cut in. She said: 'Ralph, you're wearing yourself out.'

'But I feel fine, Miss Beaumont. The fog's burnt off — not that I mind fog, it feels good on my skin — and the sun's out and the lieutenant is really a dandy driver, and we're in the country and going on a trip.'

Trip to an insane asylum for him.

Miss Beaumont said: 'You don't have to entertain us all the time, Ralph.'

That got a pleasant chuckle out of him. 'I am talking too much, I know it. It's a social fault of mine; I'm always monopolizing the conversation.'

Another Volkswagen cut out to my left, passed us, and fell in ahead of us. I said: 'Maybe the reason you talk a lot is that you know a lot, Ralph.'

Miss Beaumont gave the first really natural, full smile she'd given since we'd started. She even lifted one hand, as though about to pat me, but of course resisted the impulse, if it had been one. Ralph, on the other side of her, beamed. 'My, thank you, Lieutenant.'

'I'd really like it better if you both called me Andy.'

Ralph said: 'Now, if I'm to develop good social manners, I have to figure out some way to make one of you do some talking. How did you get into police work, Andy?'

He had me laughing, then. I said: 'You drew a blank that time, Ralph. The army assigned me to an MP company when I wasn't much older than you are now. When your father hired Jack Davis as police chief in the Vista, he wrote me; we'd been buddies in the service. I'd had enough army, and took the job.'

Ralph looked out at a line of telegraph poles that had swung in alongside the freeway. He did something that involved counting them, looking at his wristwatch and checking the speedometer of the Cad, all at one time, and said: 'The speedometer is clocking seventy-eight, but we're only going seventy-four and a half.'

Miss Beaumont said what was on my mind. 'How in the world, Ralph? You'd have to have three eyes and a calculating machine in your head and — ' She shook her head. The tam o'shanter flopped around.

Ralph said: 'Why, it's quite simple. Pole erectors always space that type of pole forty to the — No, I'm lecturing again. What made you go into psychology, Miss Beaumont?'

'Ralph, your technique is disarming. Why, I was the little girl who took the watch apart when I was a kid.'

'But everybody does that. I've taken a dozen watches apart. Dad found a jeweler who'd sell him old watches, to protect his own. Andy, didn't you take watches apart when you were a boy?'

I just shook my head. Nobody ever left a watch loose around an orphan asylum. Hardly anybody had a watch.

'That's boys,' Miss Beaumont said. 'It's very unusual for women to take watches apart. So now I want to take brains apart, it's the same thing.'

'What do you make of my brain, Miss Beaumont?'

In the rear-view mirror, a maroon car was trying to overtake me. I straightened my right foot a little and made it impossible for him. Volkswagens, yes; Buicks, no. I wasn't going to let that Cad's feelings get hurt.

Miss Beaumont was saying: 'I think you're an extremely nice boy, Ralph.'

He squeaked something I couldn't understand, and I glanced over. He had slumped in his seat next to the doctored door. There was a frown on his young forehead. He said: 'I'm never going to marry. I don't like women.'

Miss Beaumont was sliding in the seat, pushing over against me. It wasn't affection; she was giving Ralph as much room as possible. I could feel the tension in her arm and thigh. She had made a mistake, and not a social mistake, in Ralph's phrase; a professional one. Sympathy or warmth from a woman was the worst thing for him. Miss Beaumont was too near me for me to see her face in the mirror, but I knew how she'd be looking; like a police officer who was getting along fine in a questioning, and then made the one remark that would cause the suspect to shut up.

I wondered if any compliment would have made that change in Ralph. What would have happened if a man said something warm to him? There was no intention in my mind of making the experiment; I'd been paid to drive him to Kansas, not to exercise amateur therapy. But I had to say something, or we might have trouble. 'Your house help seems like a nice guy, Ralph. What's his name?'

His voice was a million miles away, out in space with the stardust. 'Sam, or something. Everybody's got a name, hasn't he? Miss Beaumont, I'd like one of those pills now.'

Miss Beaumont said: 'Of course, Ralph. Will you stop at a filling station for a glass of water, Andy?'

She hadn't called me by my first name before, but it didn't mean anything. We'd been talking about servants' names and I was a chauffeur.

Ahead there was a 'roadside business' sign and a turnoff. I let up on the gas, drifted into the right hand lane, and coasted downhill to a gas station and a pump.

Before the car was barely stopped, I was out and around the long hood to open the right-hand door. But if I thought that would be necessary to save Ralph embarrassment, I was wasting my time. He had drifted off past the Milky Way and didn't know where he was.

Miss Beaumont got out on my side and went to get water. I stood between Ralph and the curiosity of the filling-station men, and told one of them to see how much gas he could get into the Cad, to keep him busy.

The kid was not well; his lower jaw wobbled and his eyes rolled. Miss Beaumont got back fast; she'd soaked her cuff hurrying with a full paper cup of water. Her bag hung open from her shoulder, and I could see more paper cups in there. She had expected this sort of thing.

The pill worked fast; his eyes came back to the front and steadied, and almost at once began to close. I gave my credit card to the gas-pumper, and moved away to my own side of the car.

The station attendant brought me the slip to sign and said: 'The boy sick?'

I nodded, scrawling my name on the ticket.

He tore off the duplicate and handed it to me. 'My folks have a motel about a mile up the road; they'll make you a day-rate. You oughtn't to try and take a sick boy across the desert.'

'Times must be hard,' I said.

He gave me a hurt look, and turned on his heel and went back into the station. Miss Beaumont said: 'He was only trying to help.'

'I'm just a cop,' I said. 'I lack polish and finesse.'

She shrugged and came around to get in from my side. Ralph was going to sleep. She said: 'All there is to this world is the human relation. Every time you reject a friendly overture, you chisel off a piece of your own life.'

'Great thunder in the sky! A lady philosopher.'

Very primly, she said: 'Philosophy is the basis of psychology,' and slid into the car. Unfortunately her skirt caught on the edge of the seat, and slid up a good foot, and she had to grab and pull it down, which ruined the prim effect.

I decided if I whistled, she'd probably pull a gun from that useful handbag and shoot me. I didn't even smile, but got in next to her, and called to the filling station man: 'Thanks for the tip, anyway. Maybe we'll stay with your folks some other time,' and went off down the road to the east. 'See,' I said. 'There's nothing I won't do to make this a friendly voyage.'

She had fished out a plain linen handkerchief, and was mopping the corner of Ralph's mouth; he was sound asleep, his cheek against the seat cushion, making him look even younger than usual. So she didn't answer me, but she slid towards me, maybe to give Ralph and his long legs room.

'He's really knocked out. What's in that pill?'

'A very mild tranquilizer,' she said. 'But he was exhausted. When a subject has reached the end of his nervous stamina, a soda mint or a suggestion will put him to sleep.'

'Thanks, prof,' I said. 'If you're sure he's out, will you relax for a few minutes and talk like a human being? I know why you pull the Miss Priss act, but the — subject? — can't hear you just now.'

Off to the right was the old pre-freeway highway; four lanes, lined with tall eucalyptus. Behind the eucalyptus, nicely kept lawns stretched back to frame houses built in the turn of the century; wealthy small-town bankers and lawyers and fruit growers lived in them, I supposed.

I'd been watching them, and so had she, because she said: 'What'll we do, pretend we're Mr. and Mrs. and we live in one of those nice old houses? You run a mousetrap store, and when you come home at night, I'm dressed in a housecoat covered with sequins, and I have a nice elephant's-blood cocktail for you.'

'Where do you get elephant's blood?'

'Why, we keep it in the freezer. It's canned by an elephant-blood cannery in — ' She broke off and put her hand on my wrist, just below the cuff of my sports shirt. 'I'm sorry, Andy. I'm not much good at playing.'

'You've got the clothes for it. I saw them in your closet. I'd like to see you dressed up sometime.'

She shrugged. 'The body's not bad, but the face is — well, horsey.'

'Not the face, kid, just the expression. You're too damned intense is all.'

She said: 'Andy, I do believe you're making a pass at me. How nice of you!'

'All I am is a battered old policeman. You'd be a very attractive kid, if you weren't so serious.'

She reached up and put her hand on my cheek. 'I know you're just doing this because you're afraid I'm worrying. I am. I'm pretty darned serious about my profession. Most psychologists are; even the teachers I had in school, who'd been in the profession thirty years and more. It's why I chose it, back when I was just a fluff-headed eighteen-year-old sophomore. A future that wouldn't rub off and leave me cynical seemed a pretty brave project.'

If this was her idea of light chatter, it was all right with me. 'Where did you go to school?'

'U.C.L.A., Berkeley. Columbia, two

summers. I did a year as attendant at Patton State Hospital in preparation for my master's. I'm working on my doctorate now.'

This fetched the whistle I'd bottled up before. Patton was the lockup for the criminally insane. 'Attendant?'

'Yes. Bedpans and floor mop, with a little sack of sand in my apron pocket in case any of the ladies got rough. I had to use it twice.'

'You *are* serious about your profession.' The houses and the lawns and the eucalyptus trees had run out now, and we were passing through endless grape arbors: stumpy pruned-back pieces of vegetable ugliness growing in pure sand. This was the beginning of the desert. I switched on the air conditioner. We'd barely made a tenth of our trip, and the kid was already knocked out.

'Yes, I guess I am,' she said. 'Aren't you about yours?'

'Mine's a trade, not a profession,' I said. 'Three years of high school, and the army seemed to think I'd make a cop. I've been to advance training, of course, and I did take the FBI course.'

'While you were in the service? I thought the government departments were too jealous of each other for that.'

'On my own time. Accumulated leave.'

'You see?' she laughed. 'You *are* serious.' She turned and looked at Ralph. 'Out like a light. Give me a cigarette, will you, Andy? He doesn't like to see me smoke.'

'Light me one, too.'

There was the faintest trace of lipstick on the butt she handed me. I asked: 'What do you look like when you don't look like this?'

She shrugged, and answered with another question. 'Why do you keep looking in the rear-view mirror?'

'Earlier I thought we were being tailed. A maroon Buick, middle-sized, two-door. But I haven't seen it in quite a while. Guess I was wrong.'

She turned and looked over her shoulder at the following traffic. 'Why in the world would anybody want to follow us?'

There were some answers to that, but I

didn't want to worry her with them. And at the same time, I half-believed she knew the answers; all that psychology was as likely to come up with an answer as all my police experience. I said: 'Let's let it go. Too much talking might wake Ralph up.'

'Certainly.' She put the half-smoked cigarette out in the car's ashtray, and watched the grapevines go by.

I said: 'Sounds romantic; mile after mile of vineyards and grape arbors. Then you see them, and it's about as beautiful as driving through endless car-wrecking yards.'

She laughed. 'At this point, I say: 'Ah, life.''

'So say it.' A wind began to come up; the California north wind called a Santa Ana, or Santana. I played with the window controls, and Ralph's window slid up; that Cad had everything. I closed my own, too, and there was just the hum of the motor and the buzz of the air conditioner. 'I hope that air conditioner knows not to scoop up sand. This stuff's sharp enough to take the paint off your car.'

'Mr. Bartlett can buy a new air conditioner. Or a new car.'

This didn't sound like her; it sounded more like me. I said: 'Don't get bitter. Whatever Mr. Bartlett's paying you will go a long way towards that doctor's degree.'

'Of course, I don't know all the answers.' She sounded so unhappy I looked at her, taking my eyes off the road. Behind her, the grapes had stopped and the desert brush — greasewood, cholla and beavertail — was starting up. It didn't look grimmer than her face.

'Tell papa.'

'Seven years of study doesn't make a psychologist. But I've seen enough to know that a fine brain — a truly fine brain — doesn't go off its track as far as — I don't want to say a name; it has a tonic effect, and it might wake him — off its track if there's enough love and attention. And — ' She stopped, got a handkerchief out of the bag, and started gnawing one corner of it.

This wasn't going to get us anyplace. I said: 'There isn't any better clinic in the

49

world than the one we're heading for, they tell me. There's been no money spared. And talking of that, open the glove compartment and take out a little package with my name on it. It's got our expense money in it. You'd better take part of it. You don't want to come running to me if you need a new nightgown or a pair of nylons.'

Andy Bastian, the psychologist. 'I've got enough clothes with me for a week.'

'Don't be silly. The entire United States is busy padding expense accounts. If it gets chilly, you need a new sweater. If we stop at a motel with a swimming pool, you need a swimsuit.'

She laughed. 'All right, copper. Corrupt me.' She reached across Ralph's tangled legs and got the package out.

Far behind me, in the thinning traffic, I thought I caught a glimpse of Buick maroon. But I'm neither an artist nor a color stylist; maroon is maroon. I slowed down, but none of the cars that overtook us were the one.

We got to the San Berdoo bypass then and I was busy making the switch for

Cajon Pass. We headed north and started climbing. Miss Beaumont was quiet, and when I got the car headed into the wind, I said: 'What now?'

'There's five hundred dollars in cash here, far too much. And two Syrettes.'

'Morphine,' I said. 'I asked Mr. Bartlett's doctor, Martin, for them.'

'But Ralph — '

'Is never violent,' I said. 'I know.'

She put the Syrettes and most of the money back in the box and into the glove compartment. Except for saying, 'I'm taking a hundred, I'll account for it,' she said nothing more through Victorville and Barstow, and out onto the two hundred miles of glaring, naked desert that separated Barstow from Needles.

After a while, Ralph woke up and sat upright by his window, and she sat up right by him, and I lounged behind the wheel and drove, and none of us talked. Ralph looked very tired; he was getting circles under his eyes.

4

It was lunch time when we got to Needles, but no place there looked intriguing; I drove on through. We'd made awfully good time, over three hundred miles in about six and a half hours.

Hearing that they were going to eat pretty soon stimulated my passengers. I asked Ralph: 'Why isn't there a bridge at Needles? You drive down along the river and then up on the other side.'

He said: 'I don't know; I've never been here before, but I'll study the geology as we go along.'

'Fine.'

Miss Beaumont got a compact out of her bag and genteelly powdered her face. Ralph looked a little annoyed at the faint aroma of the powder, but maybe that was my imagination.

We rolled out on the bridge and across it, and were in Arizona. Ralph turned away from the window. 'I just don't understand it. They go all out of their way to cross where the river's practically a lake, when they could get over at a much narrower stand. Of course, there's more rock here, but the extra mileage would pay for a lot of hauling and concrete enforcement.'

'Wonder where we could find out?' I asked. A sign ahead said we were coming to an Inspection Station, All Cars Halt.

Ralph was musing as I slowed the Cad and turned in under the long sheds, pressing the button that opened the windows. A green-uniformed man waved me to a halt and said: 'Any plants, cotton, honey? Any agricultural material at all?'

I shook my head. He started to say, 'Please open your trunk,' as they always do, but he never got more than halfway through.

Ralph had flipped again. 'This is illegal,' he said. He had one of his bony arms out the window, was waving it at the startled inspector. 'The Constitution says you can't set up an embargo between the states, but you you people with authority, you have to, have to — '

Unlike most people, Ralph didn't get

red when he got mad; he got whiter. I was out by then, and going around the car to him. Miss Beaumont slid away from him, under the wheel. I saw the inspector start to follow me, going for the gun they carry but never use — only she caught his arm and started talking to him in a low voice.

Other inspectors were hurrying over from the other tables. Way ahead, a motorcycle fired to life, and an Arizona highway officer came rolling down to the shed, past two big trailer-trucks. The drivers of the trucks were getting out, too.

Ralph was still yelling, his voice high with what sounded like fear. Authority was the enemy of freedom, the best government was the least government, the quasi-police state stifled thought — I don't know, I'm not sure he knew; something had triggered him again, and once started, he went out of control fast.

I took his arm, the biceps small in my fingers, and said, 'Cut it out, Ralph.'

His eyes swung up at me. 'Why? Why should I? For you or — ' He was wall-eyed with whatever ghost was riding him.

'You'll get me into trouble,' I said. 'I'm not man enough to take it. Give me a hand.'

He gulped, taking this in. He ran his hands up over his sweaty face and through his already rumpled hair.

I kept my eyes on his, but I kept mine downcast a little, as though hoping he'd help me. I managed to take a squint at Miss Beaumont and the inspector she was talking to. He was looking at the handleless door and nodding.

The inspector stepped away from the car and waved the other greenshirts away, too. He put up both hands, and the highway patrolman coasted to a stop by him, holding his cycle up with one leg while it putt-putted impatiently. The inspector started talking fast; after a moment, the patrolman's head started bobbing up and down in agreement or understanding.

Ralph made it back to control. He said: 'I'm sorry, Andy. Maybe they'll let us go on and not take your name. What kind of trouble could they give you?'

'Making a disturbance in a neighboring

state would look bad on my record,' I said. 'The sheriff might even revoke my license to be a policeman.'

'Oh. Guess you need the job to live by, eh? Do you believe that economic pressure is responsible for most of the crime in the world? Many good sociologists do. On the other hand — '

'We'll talk it over as we wheel. Now, I'd like to get out of here, and thanks a lot.'

He gave me the brightest kind of smile, and let me go. Everybody stood well back as we drove out of the long cool shed into the Arizona sunlight; they didn't want any part of us.

As sun hit the hood of the Cad, shade hit the radiator of the maroon Buick pulling into the shed behind us. There was no longer any doubt in my mind that we were being followed. Anger made my hands clench on the wheel. We weren't carrying anything worth stealing; and while kidnapping the son of a man as rich as Mr. Bartlett would be a profitable venture, I've never had a taste nor a mind for melodrama.

So the only reason anyone would follow

us that I could dredge up was that Mr. Bartlett didn't trust us — me, really — to do our job, and was sending inspectors along to check up. Maybe he had inspectors trailing the inspectors; he was rich enough.

Under my breath I called Mr. Bartlett several names, some of which started with the same letter his did.

From Needles to Kingman is no great distance. On the western edge of Kingman was a Chinese restaurant that had been advertising itself along the way. I pulled in and parked, and we all got out. Ralph let me open the door for him, and gave me a comradely smile; he had helped me, I had asked for his help. I wondered if anybody else had ever done that to him; but I wasn't naïve enough to think that little minor touches like that would cure or would have prevented a deep neurosis like his. I had brought a bunch of NPs out of the combat zone in France once, and none of them had been any worse off than Ralph.

We walked into the restaurant, a very nice one, and I got my party seated at the table, asked Miss Beaumont to order for me, and at once took off for the men's room; I had to case it before I allowed Ralph to use it alone. But it was okay, with a small back window and only one door. I removed a layer or so of desert sweat that I'd accumulated despite the air conditioner, and went back to the table. I passed Ralph on the way. He still liked me, from his smile.

Miss Beaumont said: 'Could we have a cocktail?'

'You're the psychologist.'

'Not such a damned good one. I should have prevented that last blowoff, and the other one was entirely my fault, too. Oh hell, the more normal we are, the better. A martini for me.'

I told the beautiful Chinese hostess about our needs, and she went away. Miss Beaumont said moodily that she'd ordered the regular two-dollar luncheon for all three of us. 'That's what Ralph wanted. You get one extra dish for two people, three for three and so on . . . '

'You fascinate me.'

'It was you that came up with the

beauty, Andy. Asking Ralph to help you. You're a better psychologist than — '

My hand came down on hers, and squeezed. She reacted with enough surprise to make me think no man had held her hand in a long time. I said: 'Stop flogging yourself to death. You've got to know about people to do police work. Maybe when we get back, I could put you in our department for a while. We carry three policewomen, and they're always getting married and quitting us.'

'At the moment, if anybody asked me, I'd get married and quit my profession.' Then she realized how that sounded, and turned a rich Chinese red, quite appropriate for where we were. Then we both laughed, and the pretty hostess brought our martinis. Miss Beaumont said: 'Are you married, by the way?'

'No.' I sipped my drink, and made a big decision. 'Listen. Did Mr. Bartlett tell you he was having us followed?'

She looked very startled, and shook her head no.

'A maroon two-door Buick cased us while we were loading up this morning;

it's been behind us ever since.' The door of the men's room opened, and Ralph was coming towards us. 'It couldn't be anyone but a checkup man paid by Bartlett,' I said. 'Anyway, I'm glad he doesn't trust you any more than he does me. It gives me company.'

'I'll be glad to see Kansas,' Miss Beaumont said. 'And I never thought I'd be saying that.'

We both grinned at Ralph, and he sat down. I said: 'I'm sorry I can't offer you a drink, Ralph. Anything soft you'd like?'

'Oh, we get tea with the meal, there's no use spending money on anything else.' It was the first time he'd sounded like the rich boy he was. 'I've had a drink; Dad gave me a highball on my last birthday. It didn't do anything for me . . . Where's the menu?'

'They took it away after I ordered,' Miss Beaumont said. 'Why?'

'I'd like to figure out the cost of each individual dish,' Ralph said. 'I was thinking in the washroom, that's what took me so long. If they add one dish for each extra member of the party, somewhere short of two hundred people, they would only be getting a penny a portion . . . You have to make a curve; there's something periodic in the pattern that won't show up till I get a graph made.'

Miss Beaumont said: 'I'll bet you could do it easier with algebra.' She smiled at me, her professional, wintry smile. 'Andy, reach out and snag that menu off that empty table . . . Look, Ralph. Take the cashew chicken. It's common to three, no four, differently priced dinners. So using it as X, you ought to be able to work out some equations that will give you the price charged for each dish. Then, if you take the a-la-carte prices — '

I interrupted. 'Hold on. You're overlooking something obvious. As the number of dishes per dinner increases, I'll bet the size of each dish gets smaller; it would have to, unless you're assuming that the customer has an unlimited capacity.'

'You're right,' Ralph said. His eyes were bright, and even his tousled hair seemed to have more shine and vigor to it; he was completely absorbed, body and mind, in a way that few adults can achieve, and only very bright adolescents. 'Look, Miss Beaumont, Andy's hit it; before you got to a dinner for two hundred, you would reach a point where each portion was invisible. The law of diminishing returns, maybe, though that isn't really a law of pure mathematics, it's — '

Anyone overhearing us would have come to the conclusion that we were headed for an insane asylum all right; to stay there, all three of us. But Ralph was happy. The kid had escaped into a clean world of numbers and formulas, where no vile man could penetrate. Having contributed my little bit, I left that world to Ralph and Miss Beaumont; they had gone well past a guy who hadn't finished high school.

There was the maroon car to consider. Of course, it could have passed here while I was in the washroom; but the driver of the Buick had tried to stay further behind us than that; the only reason he'd caught up with us at Needles was because we were delayed too long in the inspection shed, and he'd been sucked in. Once in sight of the shed, if he'd U-turned back, the highway patrolman would have pulled him down for questioning.

I could see that road from my seat, and if he hadn't passed us, he'd have to hover on the edge of Kingman a long time; too long for his comfort. Without bothering to excuse myself, I went on out to the car lot.

It was on the side of the restaurant; I hadn't been able to park where I could watch the Cad. Not that it needed watching. I'd locked doors and trunk, and there wasn't anything in it really worth stealing.

I looked around the parking lot, half-expecting to see the maroon Buick, but of course it wasn't there. I got into the Cad, hot and stuffy from being in the sun, and ran the windows down and turned the air conditioner on, and just sat there a moment, waiting for the car to get cool enough to drive. Then I started up and drove very slowly back towards the west.

Using a Cadillac for that trip was like swatting a fly with a hydrogen bomb; I should have walked. The maroon Buick was parked less than fifty feet from our Chinese restaurant; it was in front of one of those little beaneries that manage to survive along major highways. I parked alongside the Buick and went in.

A little dump, four tables and a counter, some air stuffed with the smell of misused food, a ceiling fan to keep that air moving, a woman without a hairnet or cap behind the counter, a slightly cross-eyed guy visible through the hatch into the kitchen. Husband and wife, no doubt, owners and sole workers in the joint, probably making a little less than they could at easier jobs.

And three customers. Two men and a woman.

At once I knew I'd been wrong; my cop sense, my cop experience had led me into being too cautious. These were no checkup men from Mr. Bartlett. They looked, men and woman, like three middle-aged cheesewits; one of the men was bald, and — even indoors — had a floppy blue beret which did not quite come down to his surviving hair. The other one was as skinny as Baldy was fat, and as hairy as the fat man was bald. Neither had a firm line in his face; they looked like they'd been made of cheap wax and left too near a fire.

The woman was suitable company for them; she had a mass of reddish-black hair, a full skirt covered with embroidery and junk, a blouse that had been white and was not tucked into the skirt all the way around. She wore fifteen or twenty pounds of Navajo jewelry.

I had ordered a cup of coffee; it was foul. I drank half of it and paid for it and went back to my good Chinese lunch feeling wonderful. It was just a coincidence that the maroon Buick had been behind me all day; just a coincidence. A maroon Buick — surely a different one — had come up Mr. Bartlett's road and turned around. There'd been two men in it, but because of the fog, the distance and the motion, I hadn't been able to see their faces clearly. There had been no woman in the first maroon Buick; there was a woman in this one. Two different Buicks, a load off my mind.

I don't like not being trusted.

5

Full of good food, hot tea and mathematics, we rolled east again on 66. We had crossed the mountains that border the Colorado and were in the flat part of Arizona, the road lying straight and clear ahead of us. Ralph was busy figuring something on yellow paper he'd taken out of his inner pocket, and Miss Beaumont was sitting straight between us, her head nodding now and then. I said: 'Miss Beaumont, why don't you climb in the back and take a real nap?'

'Oh, I'll wake up in a minute,' she said. 'I'm like a snake; I always get sleepy after a heavy lunch.'

Ralph looked up from his paper. 'Do you like snakes, either of you? I know most people abhor them, but they can be fascinating when you study them enough. I mean there are hundreds of kinds, and there's hardly anything you can say about them that applies to all snakes; some even have hind legs, though they don't use them. This is sidewinder country here, you know — '

He was off; we were all off again. Miss Beaumont was wide awake now, her eyes shining; it was hard to guess if she found Ralph's mind professionally fascinating as well as just plain amazing, the way it was to me. I half-envied the doctors at the Kansas clinic the opportunity they were going to have to study Ralph. The only parallel I could think of in my trade was being the officer who, single-handed, captured a man who had kidnapped the president of the United States, assaulted the queen of England, and defrauded President DeGaulle of France. In other words, Ralph was a headshrinker's jackpot.

But me, I was there to drive a Cadillac, and I did so. Like many western states, the Arizona speed limit was not defined, except as reasonable and safe. With a clear, straight road ahead, I let the Cad out. At seventy-five, that car made no more fuss than my own car at fifty. I let the needle edge up a little more, maybe to seventy-eight, not true speed, as Ralph had found out with his telegraph poles and watch. I tried to remember whether he'd said that the speedometer registered too fast or too slow.

It didn't matter. A very high truck was coming towards me; I didn't want to go through its slipstream at this speed. I took my foot off the accelerator and touched the brake.

At once something went wrong. The car slewed to one side, and for a moment I had a windshield full of the sight of saguaro and ocotillo, palo verde and mesquite. Forcing myself not to touch the brake again, I edged the wheel around and got back on the solid white-striped black road.

The truck passed me as I eased the lever from D to L. For a little, I couldn't tell whether the slipstream was dragging us or whether the Cadillac was listing from its own ailments. But in low gear she slowed steadily, and without too much wobble; I took her along the road till there was a clear smooth place on the shoulder, and brought her to a stop.

My greatest desire was to wipe my forehead, but I was there to reassure Ralph. So I tried a smile and said: 'Little mechanical trouble.'

Ralph was frowning; between us, Miss Beaumont was the color of fine linen. The boy said: 'It acted like a tie rod. What do you think?'

I looked out. There wasn't a ranch or a store or anything else in sight; just cactus and yucca and the rest of the desert growth. Cars went by us on the highway, but they didn't seem inclined to stop. And if they did, what then? I couldn't split my party by sending one of us ahead for help.

I got out of the car and looked under it with whatever intelligence on my face happened to be there; I didn't feel very intelligent. There was no absolute certainty in my mind that I knew what a tie rod was. So I let Ralph out, hoping that this was another of his endless fields of knowledge.

It was. He got down on his knees in front of the car and said: 'Yep. The right-hand tie-rod end is all smashed.'

'Can I drive it?'

69

'Slow,' he said. 'She'll drive, if you don't go fast or change speeds suddenly, or swerve in a rush. You see, momentum and inertia would both apply in a case like that, and no telling what would happen. Of course, any driving would wear the tire down unevenly. But after all, it's my father's fault that this happened; he must have driven very fast over some very rough rocky country.' He paused, took a deep breath, and ran his hand through his hair, standing there gaunt and bony, his face raised to the Arizona sky, his clothes whipping around him every time a car sucked air passing us. 'I'm certain you haven't driven anyplace where a blow like this could have struck the tie-rod end,' he said to an invisible classroom. 'Naturally, if you had gone over a heavy bolt, and the tire had picked it up and tossed it exactly at the tie-rod end, that could have done it. But consider the location of the tie rod, and of the tire, the trajectory is virtually impossible. Only the trickiest of combinations of cross-winds and ricochet could have caused it.'

He frowned and got down again,

peering. Then he stood up and smeared his face with road grease from his right hand; the knees of his trousers were smudged, too. 'Very curious,' he said. 'That end is forged, machined and case-hardened. I wonder what kind of rock would be hard enough to deal it a sufficiently smart blow to crack it. I must write to my father when I get to Kansas, and ask him where he was. We might make an important mineralogical discovery.'

'A subdivider like Mr. Bartlett explores all kinds of rough country,' I said. 'Get in the car, and we'll creep along till we hit someplace where we can phone.'

'There's a place on the map called Somewater,' Ralph said. 'About fourteen miles ahead.'

I gaped at him as he got back into his side of the Cad. He hadn't looked at a map all day, which meant that he had not only memorized our route before we left, but had carried an odometer in his head that told him just how far we had come from Kingman.

At five miles an hour, hugging the

graded graveled shoulder, we started up again. There was no water in the car; you're supposed to carry water and extra gas and oil crossing deserts, but who bothers in a Cad on 66? From time to time, I glanced at the odometer, clicking off the miles; I was absolutely convinced that Somewater would be fourteen miles from where we'd stopped. We'd lost an hour crossing the Colorado; it was close to five o'clock when Somewater — or some place, at least — came up through the mesquite. And Ralph had been wrong, for once; it wasn't fourteen miles, it was thirteen and seven-tenths. That last three-tenths I didn't have to drive was like a reprieve in the death house.

Somewater was a two-story frame house that had maybe been painted once. Barbed wire kept roving animals out of a vegetable garden behind it; in front was a store, a two-car garage, and one of those old hand-powered gas pumps selling a brand of gas I'd never heard of. The store said it had groceries and tourists' needs, whatever they were; the garage said it fixed flats, and a mechanic was on twenty-four hour duty.

The mechanic was a lean cowboy in jeans and a torn T-shirt. His arms were freckled, and maybe his face had been once, but now it was uniformly sunbaked. He said: 'Got trouble, mister?'

'Cracked tie-rod end.'

He whistled and dropped to his knees, exposing incredibly scuffed cowboy boots repaired with glue-on soles. He stood up, swinging his hands together to knock off gravel. 'You got trouble, mister.'

'Can you fix it?'

He shoved his glance at the top of the windmill tower behind his house. 'Mister, I don't carry Cadillac parts.' There was a 'but' in his voice. 'All I can do is flag down the bus when she comes through at five. *He* can call the Cad distributor in Phoenix, if he's open at night; some parts departments are, some not. Me, I never had to call the Cad distributor before. Then, if he's open, he'll put a tie-rod end on the plane, and they'll drop it off in Kingman, an' the six o'clock bus tomorrow mornin'll drop it off here — an' I'll put her in.'

He decided the windmill could get along without supervision for a while, and looked at me. 'Then I'll put in about four bucks' worth of time putting a new end on your tie rod, and you'll be good as new.' He looked at the car. 'She is nearly new, at that. Funny she'd break, but you niver can tell.'

'And if all that doesn't work? I mean, the distributor being open, say?'

'The bus driver's my wife's brother. He'll phone in th' morning.' He sighed and looked at the windmill again. 'Ya maybe oughta give him some money fer his trouble.'

Mr. Bartlett's expense money was fat in my pocket. I peeled off a twenty and a ten and handed them to him. 'Why don't you take care of him and the rest of it?' I gave him a smile to go with the thirty. 'If you need more, we can straighten it out when the car's fixed.'

The squire of Somewater looked at the money in his hand. 'I better go hunt up a Cad book afore the bus comes through. One way or another, mister, you'll be rolling again by noon tomorrow, latest at one o'clock.'

74

'Fair enough.'

He had gone into the garage and was shuffling incredibly greasy papers around on the workbench. 'Here she is,' he said. 'They mailed me this stuff, but mostly I fix flats an' boilin' radiators.' He jerked a thumb out at the seemingly flat and bare desert. 'Ranch back there, but *they* bring a mechanic down from Seligman when one of their tractors needs work . . . Here she is.' He had a stump of pencil in his pocket, and wrote out some numbers. Then he looked at the windmill again, and stepped out to the sign that said that flats were fixed here. He pulled down a hinged panel and left it swinging, a sign to the bus-driver brother-in-law.

'We oughta git this Cad under cover,' he said. 'Sand around here's pure hell on paint, an' she's a pretty one . . . Shouldn't drive her with a tie rod loose, but since you come what you come, ten feet more won't hurt her.'

Miss Beaumont and Ralph had gone into the house, presumably to drink Cokes or such other comforts as Somewater provided. The cowboy drove the

Cad under the shelter of the garage, and came out again.

'What would break a tie rod that way?'

He looked at me and shrugged. 'Metal gets tired, mister,' he said; actually he almost said 'tard.' 'Like the rest of us. Usta work with a fella could lift the back end of a Model A up with his hands. He was drillin' a little bitty hole in a wooden handle one day, an' fell over dead.'

This increased my fund of automotive knowledge considerably. 'Can you put us up tonight?'

This was too much to be handled without aid. He walked around until he could see his windmill. It gave him the answer. 'Nope. Only one bedroom in th' house. M'daughter sleeps on the couch in the living room.' He thought a long time. 'You c'd take the bus when she comes, back inta Kingman . . . Course, that'd make it hard to get back here in the mawnin', but mebbe I could drive the Cad back there, an' you could drive me back here.'

This wouldn't do at all, of course. It was going to be necessary to take Mr.

Somewater into my confidence, a short ways. 'The boy's sick,' I said. 'I'd just as soon not take him on a bus.'

He said; 'Oh.' He looked unhappy for me, I suppose, because he said: 'Son?'

'No. The young lady with us is a sort of nurse.'

This produced an effect I hadn't expected. He said: 'Doc, leave it to me.' He looked at the windmill for orders. 'My daughter'll drive you on up the road to Cupra. Good motels there, an' you'll be as comfortable as all git out. Tomorrer I'll drive the Cad up and bring my old Hudson back here. My daughter can git a ride back with the candy truck; he's due tonight. Don't you worry about a thing, Doc.'

If letting him think I was a doctor made things easier, and kept Ralph off a bus, I was willing to be a doctor for a few minutes. I said: 'Your daughter could stay the night with us; she and Miss Beaumont could have a motel room together. She doesn't have to ride back on the candy truck.'

'Did I say candy? This is Tuesday; it's

the Coke truck comes down. Yeah, well, all right. Lissy goes to school in Cupra. She could walk right over from the motel; she'd like that.'

Mr. Bartlett wouldn't mind, I knew. 'I'll want to pay her for her time.'

'Sho, Doc, don't flip yore money around. This is an election year.'

I didn't know what that had to do with it, but I said: 'Not my money. Ralph's father would want me to pay for what we get. Anything to make the boy comfortable.'

He told the windmill that having a sick child was about the worst of all things, and then went trotting around the garage. I could hear a rather feeble battery turning over a stiff motor.

6

Lissy was really named Elizabeth; she
told us at once that she didn't like the
nickname. She didn't look like she could
possibly have been produced by the
sunbaked cowboy and the dough-faced
wife I'd seen back at Somewater. She
could have lived in Los Angeles or New
York, and never been out in the desert
except with her high-school class. Elizabeth was brunette, well-curled, lively and
sixteen years old; a junior in high school,
she said. She drove the old Hudson with
one hand, and she nearly frightened me
when she used the other one to wave
madly to an oncoming bus. 'That's my
Uncle Dan,' she screeched. 'He's been
chasing the Dog for fifteen years.'

The Dog was the Greyhound, and
Uncle Dan was the man who was going
to phone from Kingman for the new part.
He was Elizabeth's hero. 'Boy, I wish I
lived with Uncle Dan. He's got a place in

Williams. Man, oh, man that's living. If I lived in town, I could be in the school band, but I have to catch the old Yellow Fever every day before band practice starts.'

The Yellow Fever, it seems, was the school bus; an object as low as the Dog was high.

Ralph, sitting next to her on the sprung front seat, was fascinated. 'What would you play?'

'Baton,' she said. 'I'd be a drum majorette. Man, oh man, that's swinging. There's a contest every year for Drum Majorette of Arizona — the winner gets to go to the big football game at Tucson and lead the All High School band. Man, oh man, that's flying!' Her free arm twirled an imaginary baton.

Miss Beaumont was, of course, beside me on the back seat. She said: 'How long have you lived at Somewater?'

'Since I was two,' Elizabeth said. 'Daddy got the station on his GI. Man, oh man, that's a drag. Seligman or Cupra, they know how to live there.'

'How about Tucson or Phoenix?' Miss

Beaumont asked.

'That's way out,' Elizabeth said, meaning that her imagination wouldn't extend that far. 'I hear a cup of coffee cost fifty cents in Phoenix.' She whistled. 'Seligman, now, that's a town. Two movie houses! They think they're pretty smart, because they're so big, but man, oh man, is Cupra going to rub it into that big old city next fall.'

'Football?'

'You can say it again.'

It was Ralph who had asked if it was football Cupra was going to play against Seligman. He said: 'Cupra, that's a funny name. What does it mean, Elizabeth?'

'I dunno. It's Swedish or something.'

Ralph was off. 'Spanish for copper is *cobre*, and Latin is *cuprum*. I think the French is *cuivre*, isn't it, Miss Beaumont?'

From beside me, she said; 'Yes. Maybe it's Italian, *cupra*.'

Ralph said: 'Yes, it could be. And then there's a special Swiss language, Romano, that is derived very directly from the Latin. A number of Swiss moved to

Arizona in the late 1890s and early 1900s, principally to raise alfalfa and go into the dairy business.'

Elizabeth, Princess Somewater, turned her head from the wheel. 'Gol-ly! What grade are you in, Ralph?'

'Well, I've completed high school, a year ago, but my father won't let me go to college yet, so I've been studying at home.'

With the complete frankness of youth, she said: 'I'm seventeen, last June 17th.'

'I'll be seventeen October 12th.'

'I'm older than you, but you sure know a lot more. I guess that's 'cause you've been sick.'

He said he guessed so. The face under the tousled hair was turned towards her; for the first time there was color in his cheeks. He was asking her what her favorite study was, and it came out it was geometry, which I would never have guessed. He was saying that when he was a kid, he had hoped to trisect the angle, but he'd never been able to; she said she'd thought of that, too. Now you take a ninety-degree angle, and you know the answer is thirty degrees, and you work back from there . . .

Kids.

I looked over at Miss Beaumont. She was grinning a quiet grin, and, in spite of her tugged-back hair and tailored professional-looking clothes, a pretty woman was looking out at me, almost flirting with me. The same woman who had talked to me in her bedroom. She was out, like Gretel on one of those Hansel and Gretel and the Witch weather predictors. Elizabeth had temporarily eased the awful pressure on Ralph, and Miss Beaumont was relaxing under the equally awful burden on her. I reached over and took her hand and squeezed it, and she turned it over so the palm was against mine. Then she released her hand, plucked a cigarette from my breast pocket, and felt back in the pocket for a match, though she had said that Ralph didn't like her to smoke.

Elizabeth let the old Hudson swerve, and Miss Beaumont's hand came against my chest harder than she'd meant. I guess she felt the gun there, because her smile faded, and she sat back against her side of the rear seat and said: 'Could I have a match, please?'

I gave her one and let her light it herself, because it wasn't good for Ralph to be reminded she was female. We were back on the treadmill. But he didn't seem to mind Elizabeth's gender at all. They were still chattering away in the front seat about courses they'd liked in school and courses that had been a drag. Ralph was beginning to say 'Man, oh man' every little while.

Then we slowed down and pulled into Cupra. I asked Elizabeth which was the best motel. 'Goll-ee, I wouldn't know. There's an awful big one, the Glory Hole, right in the middle of town, but they say it costs a fortune.'

'Let's find it, even if the coffee's four bits a cup.'

'The town kids, now, they eat at Chris's. I was there once when Daddy let me stay in for a basketball game. It's keen . . . '

'Maybe we'll have dinner there. But find the Glory Hole.'

The Glory Hole Motel was just another

Highway 66 place: huge copper-colored neon sign, big-leafed plants in the imitation rock planters, coffee shop at one end of the arcade and office at the other, driveway to the rooms in between. But Elizabeth's eyes were shining; man, oh man, this was swinging; the city kids in Cupra (population 975) would bug when they heard she'd stayed at the Glory Hole.

She stopped the old Hudson by the office, and I climbed across Miss Beaumont's knees and got out. Elizabeth shot out ahead and stopped. 'Gosh, Doctor, you don't have to get a room for me. I mean, there's kids in my class I can stay with.'

'Elizabeth, it won't be more than a dollar more to get you and Miss Beaumont a double than to put her in a single. Be my guest.'

She gulped and nodded.

For sixteen of Mr. Bartlett's numerous dollars, I got us two doubles with twin beds, well back off the highway. They were party-walled, I found when we got back there, with a carport for our use on each side. She put the Hudson into the port furthest back, and I carried Miss Beaumont's bag into that room, my bag and Ralph's into the other.

Ralph fell on one of our beds and lay there, inert. The reaction from being with the girl set in; he looked paler than ever, and without interest in life. I scouted the room. No back door, and the small bathroom window that opened onto the fields was covered with hardware cloth. I asked him if he wanted to shower first.

There wasn't any answer at all. He lay back, his head on the bedspread covering the pillow, his eyes open, but gone; not hearing me at all. I said: 'Take a shower, Ralph. Then we'll buy your girl the most expensive meal in Cupra.'

The response was a lot more than I'd paid for. He sat up, his eyes much too bright. 'Don't you laugh at her just because her father has a crummy old garage out in a crummy old place! I wish I could live over a store and help my father change tires, and — ' He began to sob.

'Not laughing, Ralph. I just wanted to show her a good time, and so do you.'

He shrugged. But he was sitting up now, and not crying. 'Why did you let her think you were a doctor, Andy?' The key to Ralph was his curiosity.

There wasn't any answer to that that I could give him. Anyway, he was smart enough to figure it out, so I just looked at him. 'Yes, I see,' he said finally. 'Only a crazy man would have a policeman taking him to a hospital. Maybe she thinks I just have tuberculosis or something.'

'Take a shower, kid.'

He nodded and stood up, starting to undress. I turned away, looking out the front window at the motel landscaping. Hell, cops don't cry. But a kid who hopes he can pass for something real high-class like a tubercular — I had to remind myself that he had everything I had wanted back when I was in the Home. Money, a nice room of his own, books . . .

The water poured down on the other side of the door. I took my coat off, unstrapped the shoulder harness, and rolled it around the gun, then put the whole mess in my bag and stepped outside.

7

Here in the foothills of Arizona, it was warm enough for a shirt-sleeved man to lounge in the twilight. I lit a cigarette, sat down in one of the redwood chairs provided by the management, and smoked quietly. There was a swimming pool, but nobody was using it. Bats were swooping down on it to drink, and some birds I didn't know the name of. Nobody knows everything.

A door behind me opened and I turned quickly, but it wasn't Ralph; Miss Beaumont. I stood up, and she came over and joined me. 'My roommate's busy phoning all her high-school friends; I persuaded her you'd not mind the bill.'

'Mine's bathing.'

She nodded, and took the cigarette and light I held out to her. Then she moved towards a chair, changed her mind, and turned back to me. She laid her hand on my chest, just above my heart. 'I like you better without the gun.'

There was an answer to that; I made it by bringing one of my arms up and putting it around her shoulders. She put her cheek flat against my chest and let her body go a little limp, leaning on my arm. I could feel her breast soft against me, and surprisingly full; she was a lot more feminine than she dared admit.

My voice surprised me by saying: 'Take it easy, baby. It's rough duty, and I know it.'

She put her arms around me, gave me a quick hug, and moved away. I was breathing a little hard, which startled me; women and I aren't exactly strangers.

There was color in her cheeks now. 'I'm a shameless hussy, Andy. I was leaning on you, but it doesn't mean a thing.'

That got her my wickedest grin.

'Well, not much of anything,' she said. 'I must admit, hard muscles and a bony back give me a kick. To be scientific . . . Sometimes I'd like to say to hell with science, and go off on a three-day bat with a guy like you.'

'I'm too old for you,' I said.

'What are you, thirty-five? I'm twenty-six.'

'Well, truth is you underestimated me two years. Psychological flattery, and it'll get you anyplace with me. But I've been around too long and too far for a nice woman.'

'Who's nice?' she asked, and Hansel peeped out of her eyes and laughed at me. 'But I'm going to amount to something. Damn it, Andy, any woman can make herself up, practice dancing and light conversation, and hook a sucker. I'm going to do it the hard way.'

For that moment, in that place, I liked her better than any woman I'd met in years. I said: 'We're two of a kind. You don't go from an orphan asylum to a major's commission in twenty years without getting a crust. It gets kind of heavy to carry around.'

She understood me perfectly; people seldom do. She settled back into business again. Ralph's shower and Elizabeth's phoning couldn't last forever.

Swifts or swallows or something like that were coming in out of the darkening desert to swoop over the swimming pool. Miss Beaumont said: 'You were pretty nervous earlier today.'

'When I thought someone was following us. But I checked it out during lunch; I'd been spooked by a couple of coincidences. My suspects were nothing but three cheesewits that nobody'd trust and nobody'd hire. I haven't seen them since.'

She caught her lower lip between her teeth and nodded. 'They must have turned off for Las Vegas.'

'Cheesewits with money would go to Las Vegas. It was built to trap cheesewits.'

She nodded, and helped me count the night birds over the pool for a while. 'I'd like a drink,' she said. 'I suppose we can get one with dinner ... What's a cheesewit, Andy?'

This took some consideration. I said: 'Someone whose brains are protein, but not real meat?'

One of her very rare laughs got away from her. 'Not bad. Professional experience?'

'Yeah. The kind of crime a police

department like ours gets: a little marijuana smoking, a wild party while the folks are away, a chicken-drag race, if you know what that is.'

She shook her head and stood up, throwing the cigarette butt out on the parking lot. I moved to pick it up, then checked myself. She said: 'Tell me some other time. I'm depressed as hell. Let's get the kids organized and get to a restaurant.'

'And a drink?'

Miss Beaumont turned and faced me squarely. 'You don't miss much, do you, copper? I'm not an alcoholic, if it's worrying you. It's just that I'm lower than I like to be, tonight.'

'Once I heard a guy say he was lower than a deep well in Death Valley.'

'That's low,' she agreed, and moved, the fancy motel-type illumination sending bands of light up her neutral-colored suit, towards the door of her cabin.

I had not been puffing my cigarette as nervously as she had; I still had a little to smoke, though I'd started my cigarette before hers. How often I'd seen that

— when you're questioning a suspect, you give him a smoke, take one yourself, and before yours is half-done, his is burning his fingers.

There were mountains around Cupra, but the light inside the motel court blanked them out. I stared where they were supposed to be, and thought, *Good God, she was right, calling you copper! She's a suspect — of what? — because, after a long drive and a car breakdown, she's nervous, wants a drink, smokes too fast. You're off duty, Bastian; off every duty but one simple one, and so stop staring at nice women who study psychology, at cheesewits who drive maroon Buicks, at tie-rod ends that break unexpectedly. Everybody knows they don't build cars like they used to. Everybody says it, umpteen times a day, it seems like.*

Next thing, I'd be giving little Elizabeth, Duchess of Somewater, the third degree.

Ralph was dry and dressed and sitting in front of the dresser mirror, trying to do something to his hair to make it lie down. I said: 'Feel better?'

'Cleaner,' he said. 'I didn't feel bad before.'

Soft ground. *Walk easy, lieutenant.*
'Sure. Think I'll just wash up and let's eat. I'm starving.'

I went in the bathroom and doused my dry face and scrubbed at my gritty hands. His voice came faintly over the running water: 'Andy . . . Is she going to eat with us?'

'Sure.' I grabbed for a towel and used it, so I couldn't be sure I heard him make a noise of relief. I looked out, and he was knotting a tie around the collar of his sports shirt, which wasn't really necessary for a motel coffee shop on 66. Damned touching; first love, probably. A real cute pair of kids, suitable for a cover on the *Saturday Evening Post* — till you thought where he was headed and brought yourself up.

So I went and knocked on the next door. The women were ready, and we started for the front of the plant, and dinner. The two kids walked ahead of us, Elizabeth taking little dancing steps, Ralph gawking along beside her on his spindly, coltish legs. Behind them, Miss Beaumont and I paced like a pair of

94

grandparents, not touching each other, not looking at each other, with nothing to say to each other.

Elizabeth was full of it: 'And Norma says she has a whole bunch of new records, her dad has the radio station here in Cupra, KUPRA, that's cute isn't it, the name of the town only K instead of C.'

Ralph said: 'All western United States radio stations start with K.'

'I didn't know that. So Maryloo's coming over, and Shirley — she's new in town this year, and some boys, Claud and Danny and Doc, that isn't his real name, but his dad has the drugstore, and — '

Miss Beaumont turned and looked at me, her face white in the artificial light. I smiled what I hoped was a reassuring smile, and took a long stride ahead to get the door of the coffee shop open for Elizabeth. Inside, I said: 'What's all this?'

'A friend of mine, this Norma, is having a party, a slipped-disc party, with new records like, you know, and she wants I should come and bring Ralph. A boy from California, man, oh man, those rural Muriels'll be winging?'

I said: 'I'm sorry, Elizabeth. Ralph's been ill; he'll have to lie down after dinner.'

'Aw — ' She looked and sounded disappointed, but I was watching Ralph.

Day before yesterday he had torn up all the furniture because someone had done something that had upset him. Now he was being seriously crossed in what might well be the first love affair of his life, and we might end up with a wrecked motel, a deceased restaurant, an obliterated town of Cupra.

But all he said was: 'We shouldn't have left my books in the Cadillac, Andy. I don't have anything to read.'

'There are a bunch of big racks of paperbacks in the lobby. I saw them when I registered.'

'Good,' he said. His eyes got dreamy. 'Hey, you know, you could sell real bound books for the same price as paperbacks if somebody could invent a good binding machine. I've been working on one. You feed the thread and this plastic and — '

There wasn't any hostess or head-waiter; I had grabbed a table for us. There were menus on a little stand by the door I got us some and dealt them out. Ralph, completely preoccupied again, started sketching his binding machine on the back of his; Elizabeth — I watched her, amused — looked first at the right-hand column and gulped at the prices.

Miss Beaumont looked inside and said: 'Thank God, cocktails.' I had already smelled the damp breeze from a bar in the next room.

A woman who looked like an Indian came out of the kitchen door and went to get us water. As she set the glasses down, she said: 'Oh, hi, Elizabeth.'

Elizabeth looked up. 'Hello, Peggy Sue. These are friends of mine from Holly-wood!'

The waitress said: 'Pleased to know you.'

Miss Beaumont muttered 'martini' in a weak voice, and I told Peggy Sue we wanted two of them. She said: 'I'll tell the bartender, I'm not allowed to serve drinks,' and went to the door off the bar and gestured. Maybe she was too young even to go into a bar.

She came back. She was completely a high-school girl: fizzed hair, charm bracelet, bouncy walk. But her eyes had remained Indian; they did not admit the least knowledge of Ralph, who had now pushed back from the table and was lettering in on his complex drawing. Peggy Sue said: 'What'll it be, folks?'

What you can get in joints of that kind is fried chicken and fried shrimp and steak, no matter what the menu says. I made it fried chicken. Miss Beaumont said shrimp, and Elizabeth asked for the ground round platter. I said: 'No.' She blinked. 'I'm on to you, miss. That's the cheapest thing on the bill. Something fancy.'

'Well, then — chicken in the basket?'

Peggy Sue said: 'Oke,' and still didn't look at Ralph. But out of his private world, he was hungry. He said: 'T-bone, rare,' without looking up.

Peggy Sue said: 'Oke,' again, and then: 'You goin' to Norma's, Eliz? It's a slipped-disc party.'

Elizabeth said: 'Will do, mildew,' and the waitress went away.

The bartender came, took our order,

and went back into his bar. Ralph drew. Miss Beaumont swallowed nervously. It was up to me to be host. I said: 'I don't want to be an old square, if you still call us that, but what is a slipped-disc party?'

Elizabeth had been looking around; at the forest green walls, the lithographed pictures, the artificial leaves shoved in imitation moss to continue the idea of the outside planting. She said: 'Well, slipped discs are something old people get in their backs, like they can't walk. But discs are platters, you know, records, and slipped means, well, you're out of this world, slipped over the edge.'

'I see.' The drinks came then, and after looking at Miss Beaumont once more, I told the barman to bring her another. On top of everything else, that trip into Somewater had been a major drag. Then I paid for the first two, and he went away, and Ralph drew and lettered and I sipped my drink. It helped a little, but liquor had never done much for me.

Elizabeth was as good a guest as I was a host. She said: 'Norma's got a swift house over on Fourth and Old Creek, near the high school. Two baths and a cellerium.'

After a moment, I figured this must be a solarium. I said: 'Rich, huh?'

'Well, her dad has the radio station. Man, oh man, you can hear it clear out at Somewater. It comes in loud as the Phoenix and Tucson stations.' She frowned. 'I sure wish we could hear the Los Angeles stations, but we can't; something about the mountains. Norma's dad's got a set you can get Los Angeles on, but I guess he's the only one around here. But she's got her own record player, and her room's all done in white and blue. But the party's going to be in the cellar; they got a rumpus room like in the movies, and her folks said she could use it!'

'Man, oh man,' Miss Beaumont said. 'That's winging.'

Elizabeth looked at her, and then they both started laughing. I couldn't be sure what they were laughing at, but they both knew; they knew something I didn't. Increasingly, I realized that Miss Beaumont was just a college girl, ten years or so younger than me. Twenty-six, she'd said, but I hadn't been reacting. Olga, she'd said, but

I had had my mind on the job, and I didn't need first names.

Ralph looked up, blinking. 'See,' he said. 'You don't use cloth at all. The books are the boards and the thread goes in here, and then this plastic, and then there's a fan here to cool it, sharp and — ' He was showing it to me, but he hoped Elizabeth would notice.

She did. She said: 'I guess maybe you're the biggest brain I ever met.'

He said: 'Well, I try and figure things out.' He laid the menu in front of her, and with his pencil started to show her the drawing.

The bartender brought Miss Beaumont's second martini, and she gulped it before I could pay for it. He went away and she looked at me and said: 'Don't worry. That's it for tonight.'

'Okay.'

'Does that mean anything?'

'Look, don't get mad at me. I'm just a hired hand!'

'That you are. That you are.'

Then Peggy Sue brought the dishes and went away again. Elizabeth said:

'She's a Walapai Indian. Peggy Sue Cuero. She's in my class. There's lots of Indians around here.' And having said that, dived into her basket of fried chicken.

Mine came on a plate, and was to be eaten with knife and fork. Ralph put his drawing away, and started cutting his steak and putting it in his mouth while his eyes stayed on Elizabeth.

Elizabeth had finished her chicken-in-the-basket and was washing her little pink kitten-paws in the fingerbowl Peggy Sue had brought her. I said: 'Dessert, anyone?'

Elizabeth said: 'There'll be all kinds of guck at Norma's, and I get fat real easy, so no thanks.'

Neither of the others bothered to answer me. I decided the offer had included coffee, and anybody too lazy to volunteer didn't deserve coffee, so I put money on the table for a tip, carried the check over to the cashier, and we got out of there. I said: 'Let's see if there's a book worth reading in the office, Ralph,' and he nodded, and we went down the portal in a group. At the archway to the rooms, the women left us.

We were in reasonable luck in the office; they had the usual novels, but they had a line of non-fiction, too. I bought me a Western; and Ralph, for a mere fifty cents, found him a little dandy called *The Meaning of Art*, and we walked back to the rooms. The Hudson was gone; Miss Beaumont was sitting in one of the redwood chairs overlooking the swimming pool. The birds were gone, and the bats were now chasing bugs attracted by the lights.

Miss Beaumont said: 'Elizabeth's gone on to her platter party. Join me, lads.'

Ralph said: 'That's square. Slipped-disc party . . . No, thank you, Miss Beaumont. I'd just like to be alone and read.' Then his good manners asserted themselves, and he said: 'You won't bother me when you come in, Andy. I get quite wrapped up in a book.'

'Be my guest. I'm not a constant reader. Maybe I can entice Miss Beaumont into a conversation.'

She grinned like a canvas cloth splitting, and he nodded his polite nod and went into our room and closed the door. I sat down, but it was really too cold out now. I wondered out loud how high we were.

'The altitude of Cupra is 3318 feet,' Miss Beaumont said. 'My altitude is two martinis, which is not enough.'

That had to be laughed at. 'Getting cold,' I said.

'We can sit in my room.'

'Sure. He can't get out the bathroom window; it's got wire on it. I can sit in front and watch the door.'

'Twenty-four-hour duty, Bastian.'

'Sure.'

So we moved into her room. It was very neat, much neater than I had expected from two women, neither of whom, I was sure, had ever been a WAC or a nurse. I sat down in the only straight chair, pulling it around so I could look out the window. She sat in the armchair for a while, and then kicked off her shoes and sat on the bed, her legs up, her back stiff against the wall. 'I'm still cold, Andy.'

'We should have had coffee, but it was getting too sticky in the coffee shop.'

'Coffee and brandy,' she laughed. 'Did I say I wasn't an alcoholic? Maybe I just passed the line.'

I stood up and peeled off a ten-spot of

Mr. Bartlett's. 'There's a pitcher on the bureau. There's a liquor store across the highway. Go get yourself some brandy and have the coffee shop fill the pitcher.'

She swung off the bed. Without her shoes, she looked smaller, of course, but she looked much younger, too. 'Drink with me?'

'No, I can't. Anyway, it doesn't do anything for me, nothing at all. Except cut a chill, and I'm not cold anymore.'

'The hell you're not,' she said. She sat down on the edge of the bed and put her shoes on, careless with the way her skirt slid up her silk-stockinged legs. She saw me looking, and smiled. 'I've got good legs, haven't I? But you're too cold to do anything about them.'

'For some reason, I'm not reading you.'

'You could have let Ralph go to that harmless little party. He's got a long, dreary stretch ahead of him. Psychotherapy takes months and months and months. You're the big, hard, experienced police lieutenant. The — what were you, captain of military police?'

'Major.'

'You could have parked outside that Norma's house, and been ready to go in, had an excuse to go in if he got hysterical, if he — '

My fists were balling up, my stomach churning. I said: 'You're the psychologist. How safe was it?'

She stood there, tall again in her shoes, and her eyes bored into mine and then dropped. 'I don't know.'

'Go buy your brandy. We won't be needing a psychologist tonight.'

She went past me and out. I dropped down on my chair again. Till she got back, I'd use her room, because I needed to be alone.

They lied to me. Mr. Bartlett had said nothing about any trouble before Ralph tore up his room — but Miss Beaumont had been there during that tantrum, so there had been trouble before. They'd lied to me, and I didn't give a damn; I was getting well paid, and a cop of twenty years' experience should be able to handle any gawky adolescent.

I didn't mind their lying to me; but after doing that, one of them had no right to turn into a good-looking young woman and accuse me of being a cold-hearted brute to the boy.

There was no sense in waiting for Miss Beaumont. I slammed out and palmed the knob of our room, mine and Ralph's, and went in.

He wasn't in the room, and the bathroom door was open. So was the bathroom window. It was no longer covered with hardware cloth. That had been pushed out, pried loose with the wrought-iron leg of the bureau lamp, which was lying on the bathroom floor. The wire grid was lying on the ground outside. He was tall, but skinny as a snake, and he'd wriggled through that little window. I was smart, but he was smarter; he'd know I'd be watching the front door.

My cop's memory said Elizabeth had said Norma's house was on Fourth and Old Creek. The telephone book had a map in it. I found out where I was, and where Fourth and Old Creek was, and took off, on foot of course. I didn't even have a flashlight.

Down the highway two blocks, cross

the highway, climb up Fourth. A block from the corner, I thought I saw them. Two cars. Both of them had red lights on the roof. A state police car and a local police car. It said so on their sides.

8

Of course, it could be nothing. It could be neighbors complaining that the slipped-disc party had been too loud. It could be a deputy sheriff stopping a state police car to bum a cigarette. It could also be a Martian landing, and the cars could be their police escort.

I'm too big to sneak up on people, unless I belly-crawl, and I had no intention of doing that. But some people were coming down Fourth from the houses up there, and I waited, planning to join the crowd.

Before that happened, a third car came up; a panel job with a spotlight and a red side light. It pulled up, and two guys got out, in ranger-type stetsons; they were in profile, and I couldn't make out their faces.

One of them said: 'Anything for us, boys?' and his voice was peculiar; accented.

A cop got out of the state car and said: 'Dunno yet, but I don't think so. The sergeant's inside. A woman was knocked out, but I don't think she's an Indian kid. G'wan in and find out, if you wanta.'

A stetson nodded, and one of the two men went towards the house. The other one leaned against the panel truck and as he lit a cigarette. I could see he was Indian. The state officer strolled over to him and they chatted, too low for me to hear.

Girl knocked out. Ralph was peculiar about feminine attentions. Girl knocked out. Ralph had torn up a wing full of furniture. Girl knocked out. Ralph had gone out that bathroom window like a salmon going upstream . . .

This was the time to start thinking. With what? I —

A fourth car arrived. The man who hurried into the house carried a small bag. Doctor. The people from up the hill were there now. I edged into the little crowd they made. The Indian policeman and the state officer leaned on their cars and said nothing.

Then a man with the big star of deputy sheriff came out of the house and almost trotted to the state car. 'Got your radio warm, Stan? Doc wants an ambulance.'

My stomach started churning, slowly and fiercely and hot. The Indian officer said: 'My rig's got a stretcher in it we can let down. But I can't use it unless it's an Indian, or a real big emergency.'

The deputy turned. 'Bob, I didn't see you. It's an Indian woman, okay? Peggy Sue Cuero. About sixteen.'

'Yeah,' the policeman said. 'I'll get the stretcher ready. We can take her to the clinic at Valentine, or where the doctor says.'

He moved around to the back of the panel, opened the door, and started unstrapping something tied up against the roof.

The deputy turned back to the house. Halfway there, he stopped. 'Bob.' When the Indian policeman had pulled his head out of the car, he said: 'Isn't your name Cuero?'

'Yeah, that's my daughter.' He went back to getting the stretcher ready.

Shaking my head, I pulled out of the little crowd. A woman had been hurt — bad, as indicated by the need of an ambulance — and that was all I knew. Ralph could still be at the party, in which case they'd question him, and his father would want me there for the questioning. Ralph could have socked Peggy Sue and taken to the hills, in which case I ought to be trailing him. Ralph could have returned to the motel, in which case, I ought to, too.

Mr. Bartlett had hired me for two reasons. To get Ralph to the clinic was only one of them. The other was to keep the publicity down to zero. He could have shipped the boy on a plane, with or without me; but a fuss on a public carrier would have gotten into the papers. So he handed his Cadillac and his son over to me, and he couldn't have made a worse choice if he'd written to a mail-order detective school and asked for the phone number of its latest graduate.

There was nothing I could do now about finding Ralph if he was in the hills. I didn't even have a flashlight. If I barged into Norma's house, and Ralph wasn't a suspect, he'd become one as soon as I showed myself.

So I turned and legged it back to the motel. It was a cool night, but I must have hurried, because I was sweating as I swung in under the arch. There were lights in both our rooms; I chose the men's side first, opened the unlocked door, and peered in, not expecting to find anything.

But I did. I found Ralph, undressed and in bed. And asleep, sound asleep. I put my hand on the pile his clothes made on the floor, and found what I'd expected: the clothes were warm.

I lit a match and held it down near his eyes and he didn't flinch. He was really asleep, but that didn't mean a thing. A kid as nervous as he was — to put the best name on it I could — would have a massive reaction; if he'd committed an act of violence, he'd be very likely to go right off into a coma when he hit the safety of a bed. Or so I thought. But I didn't have to think. I had a graduate psychologist right in the next room.

I closed the bathroom window, though

there didn't seem to be any likelihood of Ralph back-dooring me again. On second thought, I reopened it and put a glass so it would break if he opened the window, break on the hard rain-washed gravel under the window. I ought to be able to hear that. Then I went and knocked on Miss Beaumont's door.

She opened the door at once and said brightly: 'Oh, you're back.'

'Back?' That was me, the man with the bright conversation.

'I knocked on your door before, but you and Ralph were gone. I figured he got restless and you took him for a walk.' She gestured behind her. 'I got a half pint of cognac and some coffee, but the coffee's cold now and — ' She stopped and stared at me. 'What's happened? Come in.'

She had changed her clothes; she had on a soft flannel wrapper, and she'd let her hair flow down her back. She had on bedroom slippers.

'Miss Beaumont, we may be in trouble.'

'Oh, cut the Miss Beaumont. I'm out of uniform now.'

I went to the bureau, poured a glass of the cold coffee, and swallowed it. It was almost unbelievable that all that had happened had not taken long enough to make the coffee ice-cold.

I told her all about it. In the middle of telling, she went and sat down on the edge of one of the beds, crossing her knees. The flannel robe fell open on her shins; she had taken her stockings off, too. There was a strangely intimate air to the scene, though she was modestly enough dressed, and the beds were made up, the room neat and orderly. I finished the telling.

She stared at a reproduction of a Van Gogh print on the wall. 'Forget it and go to bed, Andy.'

My eyes must have pictured my amazement.

She shook her head. 'So Ralph ran around in the night for a while. But he didn't hit Peggy Sue Cuero. Or any other woman. Or anybody. He's incapable of violence.'

'How the hell do you know?'

She grinned suddenly. 'Didn't I sit

right in the middle of all his destruction, and didn't everything he threw at me miss?'

'So he's a poor shot.'

She said gently: 'Don't yell at me, Lieutenant. Modern policemen don't use the third degree.'

'That's what you think . . . you can't be sure. You may be the most learned psychologist in Cupra, Arizona, but you're still a student in Los Angeles.'

'Student with two degrees. Bachelor's and master's.'

'And you expect me to pin my whole damned career on that?'

She jumped up from the bed and strode over to stand in front of me as I perched on the straight, flimsy motel chair. 'Ah, ha! Now we get it. The materialist point of view. What's in it for me! Now we get to the nub of Andrew Bastian, the ambitious man. We — '

I was thinking, *Who's screwy now? which one should I leave at the clinic, if I ever get that far?* I might have said something real good, but just then headlights hit the window of the room, with a glimmer of red over them. So I shot out my hand and clamped it over her mouth, and told the eyes glaring at me over the hand: 'Let me do the talking.'

She twisted loose, saw the lights and nodded, while I wiped my hand on my handkerchief; I'd gotten most of her lipstick on the palm. Then it came: the rapping on the door that is like nobody else's rapping; the way I rapped myself on duty.

Miss Beaumont looked at me, and I nodded, and she opened the door. It was a whole delegation of law, state cop, deputy sheriff, Indian patrolman, and our girl from Somewater, Elizabeth.

Miss Beaumont played it just right. She said: 'Oh, hello, Elizabeth.' And then: 'What's the matter, dear?' Elizabeth had been crying.

Elizabeth said: 'Peggy Sue — you know, she waited on us at supper — she's hurt.'

I looked over her shoulder at the Indian patrolman. One of the two Indian officers I'd seen out in the night had been the little waitress's father; but I couldn't tell from this man's face if he was the one.

The time had come for me to operate. I pushed forward. 'Hurt? Run over, Elizabeth?'

She began to cry too hard to say anything. The man in the state uniform said: 'She was just getting to the kid's party, the way we figure it. Or she could have been there and gone outside with some boy. Big party, the kids was thinking about themselves . . . Anyway, somebody beat her up so bad that Bob's partner, here, and the doc have gone off to the clinic with her, Code Two, I mean, sirens and red lights open . . . We got some questions to ask you, Doc.'

'I'm not a doctor,' I said. Then I managed to grin. 'Come on in, men.'

They trooped in, three big men and little Elizabeth; the men were so big they gave the impression of a whole platoon crowding in. Miss Beaumont, on duty, got an arm around Elizabeth and led her into the bathroom at the back of the room. The three men stood looking at me. The deputy said: 'You told the girl there you was a doc.'

'She jumped to that conclusion. I let her.'

The two white men were staring at me with real hatred; the Indian officer was just staring at me. All three of them had big guns, rural types, ready to their hands; my shoulder holster and Detective special were in the other room in my bag. Not that I felt any need of a gun or the desire to use one; just that for once I had an idea how the man on the other side of the desk feels.

The highway patrolman said: 'Got any identification, mister?'

Very carefully I pulled my wallet out. I wasn't worried about the state man doing something impulsive, he'd be a trained police officer, but a deputy in a dreary county could be just anybody; I don't trust amateur cops.

The patrolman looked at my I.D., grunted, and then passed it on to the deputy; the Indian officer looked last. 'You're pretty far from your jurisdiction, Lieutenant Bastian. I'm State Patrolman Nilsen, by the way. Deputy Harry Gruder. Indian Patrolman Bob Cuero.

You got any way of proving that's your card?'

'Take my fingerprints and wire them to Naranjo Vista. Or to Washington. They're on file both places.'

Nilsen ran his fingers down his jaw. 'Doubt if any of the three of us is up to such fancy telegraphing.'

Harry Gruder, the county man, shoved forward. 'The Cadillac at Somewater is registered to Sidney Bartlett.'

I was uneasy and off balance, and I wasn't used to being that way. I made my move to dominate the situation, as a police lieutenant and a MP major should. 'Listen, this is a lot of muscle to break into a man's room at night. Any possible chance one of you wants to accuse me of beating up girls?'

Harry Gruder said: 'There's sure a lot of things about you I'd like cleared up.'

Bob Cuero, surprisingly, laid a hand on Gruder's khaki sleeve; the hand and the sleeve were about the same color. 'Take it easy, Harry.' Cuero was holding my I.D. card; he handed it back to me. 'You sure look like a policeman, Lieutenant.'

Things were going better. 'Grab what chairs you can, boys, and I'll take the bed and we'll talk this over.'

Gruder said: 'We're sure lucky to have a big-shot California-type cop to tell us what to do.'

So I'd played it too hard; I'd have to tone down. A gambler in his ten thousandth hand of stud couldn't have been more tired than I was. Peggy Sue was forgotten, and Ralph, Mr. Bartlett and Elizabeth and Miss Beaumont; I was just doing what I'd been doing all my life. I said: 'Deputy Gruder, you don't look like a man who'd wait to be told to sit down.'

He grinned: 'Okay. No use getting hairy, I guess.'

Nilsen said: 'We're all officers together. Now, Lieutenant, believe me, you are going to have to clear up a couple of things. In the first place, while Bob Cuero here's the only federal officer in the place, we're all interested in this morphine that's in the Cadillac you drove to Somewater.'

I'd almost forgotten the two Syrettes I'd left in the glove compartment. I said:

'It was given to me by a licensed physician.'

'Which tells us absolutely nothing,' Nilsen said.

'No, it doesn't, does it?' That was me, making a grave noise as if what I was saying meant something. 'Maybe if I knew why you came over here, we could save time. You're not calling everybody who rented a room in Cupra tonight, are you?'

Gruder made a face as though he were going to spit. He restrained himself, though; perhaps because the owners of the motel voted in his county.

Nilsen said: 'There was a kid's party tonight. Every kid there was from the local high school; they all knew each other, never had any trouble but kid trouble. All of them except one, a boy named Ralph something or other, who's traveling with you, according to Elizabeth Gotch.'

I hadn't known the Princess of Somewater's last name before. I said: 'That's right. Ralph Bartlett.'

'He come to the party for a while, acted funny, he left,' Bob Cuero said. 'You see, we gotta ask questions.'

I looked at him. What I knew about Indians could be put in a saloon picture of Custer's last stand. There's usually one in every army company, always called Chief, and usually quieter and neater than the other boys. But I'd never known any of them well; never even bothered to ask them what tribe they came from.

This guy was something. His daughter was badly hurt and barreling through the night in an ambulance, but you'd never know it from his face. He was just a very courteous officer trying to get information. Still, the fact that he'd stayed behind — where a civilian father would have gone with her — told me he was my kind of officer. He was going to get the criminal, and leave the doctoring to the M.D.

Playing it easy, I said: 'Ralph's asleep next door, in the room he and I share.' I flipped a thumb at the bottle of brandy. 'Miss Beaumont and I were going to have a nightcap. Any of you care for a slug?'

They all shook their heads, though the deputy's lips moved as though he'd really like one. Nilsen kept to the point. 'This

Miss Beaumont, now. Elizabeth got the idea she was kind of a nurse, but since you turned out not to be a doctor, that probably falls through, too.'

'She's a college student. I'm driving her and Ralph east, to study.'

Deputy Sheriff Harry Grader was still the loud one. I could feel more drive in both the state patrolman and in Bob Cuero, but they were both enough like me for me to feel I could handle them. But the deputy was restless, and violent, and moved by something that didn't move the others, something beyond routine. He said: 'This joker's giving us a runaround. I'd like to know, Nilsen, who's in charge here. You, me, or Santa Claus.'

Nilsen looked at Bob Cuero before he answered. He said, finally: 'It's your county, Harry. The reservation line comes close to town. If the beating was done in town, it's yours; if in Indian country, it's Bob's. It doesn't become mine till you request the state to take over. You know that.' He turned to me. 'You'll have to pardon Harry. He's running for sheriff this year. It makes him ambitious to be a hero.'

So now it was decided. They couldn't have Ralph. I had been paid to take him to a clinic in Kansas, and that was where he was going. If I thought he had attacked poor little Peggy Sue — and this was the first time that pity came into it — I could tell them so at the clinic, and surely they had violent wards for people like him.

But absolutely nobody would be served by dishing him up to a publicity-crazy politician, a politician in a cop's uniform, as so many deputies are. Society would gain nothing from having Ralph in an Arizona state institution instead of in the private one his father was sending him to. In all probability, the state of Arizona would release him to the private clinic once they had him.

So I didn't even take a deep breath; I just quietly made up my mind to step outside the law. It would be a change, after twenty years.

9

A knock on the bathroom door brought Miss Beaumont out. I had no way of knowing how much she'd heard, but she was smart. We could do it by ear. I said: 'Miss Beaumont, we'd better come clean with these officers. They can be trusted. They're all loyal Americans, I know.'

She said: 'I'd be glad to talk to them, but I've got Elizabeth on my hands. It's been a horrible experience for her. I've washed her hair — very soothing — and given her some sleeping pills. I'd like to put her to bed and leave her alone.'

Harry Gruder said: 'We could talk outside. This time of year, our climate here's like honey at night.'

Nilsen said: 'Nobody except Bob here even votes in your county, Harry.'

'We'll wait outside,' I said.

Miss Beaumont said: 'I won't be a minute,' and turned back to the bathroom.

'Wait a minute,' Nilsen said. 'The girl said you were a nurse. The lieutenant says you're not. Now you talk like one.'

'I'm a psychology student. I've worked in a hospital as part of my study.'

Nilsen looked at me. He was a trained man — he didn't show any more in his face than I do — but I could read a little there; suspicion and a beginning of understanding. But we all went outside.

Harry Gruder said: 'I'd like to see this boy that all the talk's about.'

There wasn't any sense in making him madder than he was. I opened the unlocked door of our room. Ralph was still on the bed, sound asleep. Gruder grunted and went into the room fast, picked up one of Ralph's shoes, and held it up. 'Cut grass on the sole. Cooke, where that party was, is the only guy in this town can afford a lawn.'

Nilsen said: 'Only private guy, Harry. There's the motel here, and the bus station, and the post office.' He shook his head. 'Anyway, we know he was up at Norma Cooke's party. Stop playing detective.'

I said: 'Let's go breathe some of that honey of yours, Deputy.'

We stood outside, politely juggling cigarettes at each other. Miss Beaumont came out and quietly closed the door behind her. 'She'll sleep now. What happened? She said something about a girl getting hurt at the party.'

'The Indian girl who waited on us at supper,' I said. If Bob Cuero wasn't going to claim her as his daughter, I couldn't do it for him. 'She was beaten up. It seems Ralph was up at the party for a while, and they want to question him.'

'I don't know,' she said. For the first time, I noticed that she'd twisted her hair back into the tight bun again. 'The government men said he wasn't to talk to anyone until he got to where he was going.'

'And where's that, Miss Beaumont?' Nilsen's voice was very quiet.

'Someplace in Kansas,' she said. 'You don't need to know just where.'

'I'm afraid I do.'

I got her cue, though it seemed to me she was overplaying. Our bluff could be

128

easily called; the thing to do was not to push it to that point. But we hadn't had any rehearsal time. 'Let's say it's a government installation,' she said, 'and let it go at that. All this is silly, in a way, since Ralph couldn't have had anything to do with your case, but I can see how we might look suspicious to outsiders. You must be very conscientious law officers to have found out about us at all.'

But only Harry Gruder took that; the lug was simple-minded. Nilsen remained cold and alert, and I didn't have an inkling of what was going on in Bob Cuero's mind.

Gruder said: 'Well, it's a weirdie. Of course, you folks wouldn't crack the tie-rod end on a new Cadillac at a place like Somewater over in the next county, just to get to stay at Cupra just so the kid could go to a party, just — yeah, I can see you're on the level.'

But Nilsen, who was not inimical at all, wasn't friendly; he was just a cop. He said: 'A police officer, a psychologist and a kid who — what'd Elizabeth say? — acted funny. It could add up to

129

something that meant something. I don't quite see what else it could add up to. But I don't see why you'd hold out on us, Lieutenant, and that's a fact.'

'If he *is* a lieutenant,' Harry Gruder said.

Nilsen sighed. 'I ought to have that by now.' He walked away from us and to his car, parked in front of the women's motel cabin. He got in, and we heard the hum as his generator warmed up, and then his voice on the two-way, firm and confident; the call letter routine, and then: 'Mike, you got an answer from that California call yet?'

'Right here, Nil. Chief o' police, Naranjo Vista to A.H.P. Bartlett car lent to Lieutenant Andrew Bastian, Naranjo P.D. Description of Bastian follows: Six feet two, approx. 180 lbs . . . '

Harry Gruder, listening with us, said: 'I woulda made you nearer 190, loot.'

Bob Cuero grunted. Nilsen was making his thanks and signoffs in the car; the generator hum cut out and he rejoined us. 'The owner says he lent you the car. I guess that's all clear.'

Gruder said: 'Let's get going. Our man could be clear over the hills now.'

Nilsen said: 'Yeah, yeah. Harry, I'll make our apologies to the lieutenant here, and you better start your search.'

Harry Gruder went hard-heeling towards the front of the motel. I suppose his cruiser was there; at any rate, I heard a starter, and he was gone. Nilsen said: 'You going, Bob?'

'If Harry needs an Indian tracker, he better get my partner. I'm a highway Indian.'

I saw Nilsen's hard face turn and stare at Bob Cuero for a minute; then the state policeman grinned a little, but not a happy grin. He said: 'Sure, Bob,' and then turned it on me. 'No offense now, Bastian, but the way I hear, some of these new California towns, the police department is practically a private watchman service. A Cadillac less than a year old — that means money. I want a straight answer, and I think you'll give it. Are you taking this kid out of California to remove him from prosecution?'

He had come so close I could hear the

131

bullet clipping hair off my neck. 'No.' I let the single word roll around in the night. 'I've got a badge in my wallet, and I'll give you an oath on it. I don't have a Bible, but if you do, trot it out. No. There's no California law looking for Ralph.'

'You've gone to a lot of trouble to keep us from talking to him.' Nilsen wasn't smiling at all. 'Not that I'm calling you a liar, Bastian.'

We were on our way out now. I had given Miss Beaumont a clue through the bathroom door, she had fed it back to me, and all I had to do now was give it a little push, and we were out and running — as soon as our Cadillac was fixed. My mind was making a map of the southwest. Coming back, we could go through Colorado and Utah and Nevada and miss Arizona altogether. Once we had the Cad back, I could hit the New Mexico line in about six hours, and we'd never have to be in Arizona again.

Of course, it's easy to extradite on a felonious assault charge, but Ralph would be in the hands of the Kansas screw-tighteners and —

I said: 'There's some security involved. Put a genius kid together with a psychologist and the answer's one anyone can figure. But you're a plain cop like I am, Nil — ' I was pushing to use his nickname, but I had to push. ' — and two bits'll get you two bucks you can't make any more of it than I could.'

He churned this over, as I would have in his position, and threw out everything but the one word. 'The kid's a genius?'

'I guess you'll have to talk to him. I'll wake him up.'

Nilsen said: 'I don't want to shove my hard nose into anything that's federal, but I'll be there when you wake him.'

So we went into our cabin together. Nilsen stood by the door, and I shook Ralph gently by the shoulder, praying he wouldn't come out of sleep with something wild in his mouth, but not at all sure. He came up sweetly though, smiling and saying: 'The car fixed, Andy?'

I said: 'No. But a friend of mine here, Patrolman Nilsen, has something wrong with his radio. His police radio, Ralph.'

That word 'police' was all the warning

I'd be allowed to give him.

He sat up, mussed his hair up more, if possible, and looked at Nilsen. 'Oh. Arizona Highway Patrol. Let me see. I'm pretty sure your radios are all Hallicrafter-built, or Vanguard. There used to be some Sonars here, too. It doesn't matter too much. They're all six-crystal sets, pre-calibrated. You'd have to have tools; there should be a four-ohm impedance and a separate eight-ohm, and I'd have to test. But still — '

'Ah,' Nilsen said, 'to hell with it. I'm due for a night off, anyway. I'll drive her into headquarters and have the mechanic check her.'

'That would be best,' Ralph said. 'Still, I could run over some of the obvious parts, like the transformer and the mike and all — '

'Don't bother, kid. You get your rest.'

We went outside again. Nilsen was grinning in the light from the door lamp. 'I see what you mean.'

'Let's go back in. Tell him there's a wild animal loose in the night, and he'll give you a list of possible animals living at this altitude in Arizona and how to tell their

134

teeth apart. Or — '

'I got enough, Andy,' Nilsen said, and now, of course, we were all the way through the barrier. He cleared his throat, looked cautiously over to where Bob Cuero and Miss Beaumont stood near the state cruiser. 'I don't want to pry around, like I said, but — if I said electric brain, would you know?'

'Small ones,' I said, 'that go into orbit. I think. I don't know enough to break security; I'm just a bodyguard.'

'Jesus,' said State Patrolman Nilsen, 'the age we live in. When I first joined the department, we had a lot of horse-stealing to worry about. G'night, Andy.' He walked hard for the car. 'G'night, miss. Sorry to bother you. C'mon, Bob.' He scooped up the Indian patrolman, they got into his car, and they were gone. And I was alone with Miss Beaumont.

She took my arm in both her hands, and said: 'You were wonderful, Andy.'

I wanted to shout, to yell, I wanted to hit her. But I'm a trained man. I kept my voice and my hands and my temper down and said: 'Wonderful. After twenty years of being a policeman, I'm on the other side. I'm covering up for a criminal.'

She let go of my arm and stepped away from me. Her careful veneer, which cracked when she was happy, shattered completely when she was mad, I learned. 'You think Ralph's a criminal? An assault and battery case?'

'Not premeditated. He didn't mean to hit the girl. Maybe he didn't even know he was going to hit her a second before he did. But he's dangerous, not guilty because of insanity.'

'No!'

'Yes. The tearing up the house, the act in the inspection shed; those are not the doings of a mild eccentric. Maybe I haven't got your education, but I know a nut when I see one.'

She stood there looking at me as though I'd turned into a cobra. 'So all you were doing was lying so Mr. Bartlett would be sure to pay whatever he said he'd pay you.'

I watched the highway through the arch. The big diesels had the road this late; private cars were getting scarce.

'There's no use trying to explain to you why I did what I did. Why the hell should I? You're nothing to me but another hired hand on a job that'll be over in a couple of days; sooner if I can help it.'

'Look at me.'

'Those trucks out there are prettier.'

She came around and got between me and the highway. I had to look at her. To my amazement, she was grinning all over, her teeth reflecting the night light. She said: 'You've done a decent thing, and you're ashamed of it. You think Ralph beat that woman, but you don't want him pushed through a trial, and maybe knocked off balance for life. Right?'

'Miss Beaumont . . . '

'Olga.'

Somewhere behind her, a door opened and closed. I looked that way, squinting through the night. A man wandered out into the area near the pool and stood, wavering. 'Just a drunk in the night,' I said. 'Ralph ends up in a sanitarium, one way or the other. I'll have to tell the screwdrivers in Kansas about this, though.'

'Andy, you shouldn't use words like

screwdriver and headshrinker. A little respect for my profession.'

The drunk stepped in front of a light and became a silhouette. I said: 'I'd give anybody's job the respect it has coming. If you continue this business of knowing Ralph didn't do something because he has a non-violence fixation, you're a headshrinker, screwdriver and skull-tapper.'

'Mad again?'

My God, she was flirting with me! I said: 'You keep forgetting there's been a bad crime committed. We're accessories after the fact. Until I get us out of Arizona, I'm not going to feel playful.'

The flirtatious air left her and the smile went off her face. 'Andy, when the car is fixed, do this: let me drive Ralph the rest of the way, and you stay here.'

The drunk was wobbling towards the swimming pool now. I thought maybe I ought to go and stop him, but I wasn't patrolling the motel. I said: 'That's about as screwy as everything else you've said.'

'No.' She took my arms in her hands again. 'No, I've never been more in earnest in my life. You've made something

138

very admirable of yourself, Andy. You've spent twenty years building yourself into a law officer, and that's just fine. You've got to stay here and find the real criminal, to protect your façade.'

'My what?'

'The image you've made of yourself. It's the most important possession a person has.'

She was on the level. It was kind of a touching thing. I said: 'Little mother of all the world. Mother of Ralph. Mother of me. Is that the façade you've built for yourself?'

'Yes . . . What was that splash?'

'A drunk just fell into the swimming pool,' I said. 'Let's stroll up that way and give him a hand out.'

She shrieked with laughter; I put a hand over her mouth. After, all it was the middle of the night, and motel guests have a right to sleep. When she got control, I let her mouth go, and she said: 'You're wonderful. Any other man I've ever known would have galloped up there like a trackman.'

'Drunks usually sober up when they hit

water, and anyway, it takes about three minutes to drown. If he swallows a little water, it'll bring the liquor up.'

'Three minutes is long enough to kiss me. I'd like that.'

But when I put my lips on hers, her mouth kept twitching with laughter, and it wasn't much of a kiss. But I enjoyed it.

10

She was still laughing as she walked alongside me up towards the pool. The lights had been dimmed for the night, but they were bright enough to show a fully dressed man floundering around. He was in the shallow end, but he had what looked like crepe rubber soles on his shoes; he kept slipping and falling down. I guessed that the water hadn't sobered him completely.

There was a hook on a long pole resting in clamps on the fence. I held it out to him, and slowly guided him to the steps. He let go of the hook there, went up one step, and went flat on his tail. I let him figure it out; there wasn't enough water there to come up to his neck when he sat.

He finally took advantage of the steps and railing and came out to dry land, slipping and sliding on the pool edge. 'Take off your shoes,' I said, 'and don't shake water on us.'

'Who yuh orderin' around?'

'You're welcome. I only saved your life.'

'Yeah.' Whatever that meant, he sat down in a beach chair and pulled the shoes off. They had crepe rubber soles all right, the worst possible thing to walk in when they get wet.

He dangled the shoes in his hands for a while, and then solemnly threw them back into the pool. They had betrayed him and he was punishing them, banishing them to outer space. Then he looked up at me and grinned. 'You pulled me out.'

I said: 'Yes,' slowly. I had seen him before. He was one of the three cheesewits in the maroon sedan; there had been two men and a woman, and this was the man with the bald head, the little roly-poly who had been wearing the floppy beret when I gave them the check-over in the lunchroom back at Kingman.

They hadn't made any mileage at all since lunch, but they had looked to me like people who'd never make anything, completely ineffectual jerks. He said:

'Wonder if you can get a drink in this dump at this hour.'

Miss Beaumont started to say something starting with 'I' but I cut in: 'You need a drink like you need another dunking in the pool. Go to bed.'

'Who do you think you are, a cop? My old man?'

'I'm the guy who pulled you out of the pool.'

'What pool?' He sat there, dripping water through the webwork seat of the chair, looking disconsolate. 'I lost my woman. She's making out with a tough guy. That's all women want, is hard muscle an' hard talk.'

Miss Beaumont rushed to the defense of her sex. 'That's all soft women want. Try one with a few guts sometime.'

He paid no attention to her. 'I need a drink. I could catch my cold of death.' Which, for a slip, was pretty good.

He started to get up. I pushed him back into the chair, and he said: 'Take your hands off me, copper!' clearly and almost un-drunkenly. I did, and was glad, because he wandered only a few feet out of the pool enclosure before bending over and throwing up a gallon or two of alcoholic-smelling water. Maybe I'd been about to resent his insolence to the man who'd saved his life, but now I just said; 'Oh, hell,' and started for my room.

Miss Beaumont caught my arm. 'You can't leave him out here, dripping wet, in the cold.'

'It's not that cold.'

'It's fifty or less. He'll get pneumonia.'

'He'll get a cold of death,' I said. 'You heard him. I've got plenty of problems of my own without nursing drunks.'

'Please help me get him to his room.'

'God knows, Miss Beaumont, what's going on in his room. He's traveling with another man, and a slob of a woman; you heard him, she started out as his woman and she's switched.'

'To the hard guy,' Miss Beaumont said.

'Comparatively speaking. Next to Baldy there, chocolate pudding'd be hard.'

Miss Beaumont, little Miss Nosey, came around and faced me. 'You know an awful lot about them.'

'Earlier I thought they were following

144

us. They've got a maroon Buick that kept showing up on our tail.'

'Are these the ones?'

'That I checked up on at lunch. The other two don't look any better than our soggy friend there.' I looked over. Baldy had gotten back to the sun chair and was sitting with his hands between his legs, looking miserable. He was blinking, closing his eyes easily, opening them the hard way; he'd be asleep in a moment. 'You can see from looking at him, nobody sent them to follow us. Three nothings in a maroon car.'

'You've got to help me get him out of the night, or into dry clothes.'

'Miss Beaumont, you're a nuisance.' But it was easier to do what she wanted than to stand there arguing. I went along the line of rooms till I found the maroon Buick in the stall of Number 11, and then came back, walking harder-heeled than I had to, to the pool. Miss Beaumont trotted after me.

I hooked a hand under the wet armpit and hauled Baldy to his feet. 'Bedtime, mister. Sack time.'

He tried to twist away; if he'd suc-
ceeded, he would have heaved himself into
the pool again. But, of course, he couldn't
get away from me. His free arm flailed
around, and I captured it by twisting the
cloth of his cuff. Water squirted out between
my fingers. Miss Beaumont was right; that
wet and that drunk, he'd get hospital sick
if we left him out.

I let him go, caught him again by a
handful of belt and wet jacket, and
frog-walked him towards Number 11. He
said: 'Damn it, cop, lemme go.'

'Sack time,' I said again. I usually refer
to myself as a cop, which is okay; but I
don't like other people calling me that.
He'd done it three times now, on no more
authority than that he thought I talked
like a policeman.

There was grass, and there were gravel
walks, and there was the paved driveway.
Annoyed, I chose the gravel walk, pushing
him along on his shoeless feet. I hoped
the humane Miss Beaumont wouldn't
expect me to skin-dive in the pool for his
shoes; if she thought of that, I was likely
to push her in to get them.

He was sober enough to feel his feet hurting him; he said so, louder than the hour called for. I started to put my left hand over his mouth, but it was too late; the door of 11 opened, and a woman called, without consideration for sleepers: 'Skippy, where are you?'

I snapped words at her in my official voice. 'Madam, be still. If this thing is called Skippy, I've got him.'

She said, still loud: 'Oh, God, Morgan, the cops have Skippy.'

'One thing about you, Andy,' Miss Beaumont contributed, 'you'd be a failure as an undercover man.' She started to laugh her low chuckle. 'I'd love to hear you making love to a woman: Easy ma'am. Just let me have a simple yes or no: do you love me?'

'Very funny.'

The skinny guy appeared behind the woman in the door of 11. All he had on were his slacks. The dame was in a slip, and since she was standing between the lights and me, this didn't do much to conceal her; but if Miss Beaumont was anxious to hear me making love, she wasn't likely to be satisfied just now. The semi-naked dame did not exactly arouse passion in me.

I shoved Skippy at them, and the guy she'd called Morgan caught him automatically. He pushed him away. 'You're soakin' wet, Skippy.'

'He fell into the pool,' I said. 'If you want his shoes, he left them there, in three feet of water. He was mad at them.'

Morgan stepped out of the door. He had a raspy voice. 'I thought you said the law had him,' he told the woman. He turned to me. 'What are you doing with him?'

'I pulled him out of the water. Split him open, and if there's a pearl in him, it's mine.'

Skippy was nothing but a slob; this Morgan had some rough to him. He came into the light and faced me, cocking his head up so he could push his jaw out at me. 'I've seen you before, hard guy. You was checkin' us at chowtime. You got credentials for that sort of stuff?'

His lips didn't move when he talked. I made him from that: ex-convict. The other two were not; they were artists or writers, or they made clay pots or hand-dyed cloth. It's fashionable for the arty slobs to take up with convicts and hoodlums these days.

I looked over at the dame in the doorway. 'Lady, you better keep your handbag under your pillow if you're letting this hood in your bedroom.'

She put her hand to her mouth as though I had shocked her, and she stepped out of the doorway towards me. This gave me a full view of the inside of their room. It was disgusting, if anything can disgust a cop of twenty years' experience. Two beds, a double and a single, both mussed, both used. Clothes all over the joint, men's and women's mixed. You could reconstruct what had been going on in there, but after you'd done it, it wouldn't be good for anything but a chapter in one of Miss Beaumont's schoolbooks.

Behind me someone yelled, and I turned fast, wishing for the gun I'd left in my overnight bag. It was Ralph. He'd wandered out in the night, and what he saw he didn't like; and when that boy didn't like something, he, as Miss Beaumont would say, reacted. With non-violence, sure.

My hand was over his mouth and my arm was hugging the wind out of him before he waked up people outside the state of Arizona, at least; the New Mexicans, the Californians and the Mormons in Utah did not have their sleep disturbed, due to my speed and vigilance.

Miss Beaumont came after me and opened the door of the room Ralph and I were supposed to share. I wrestled him in and she shut the door. I let him go; it would be a moment or so before he got his wind back.

He sort of crumbled on the bed, and kept rubbing his hands up over his face and into his hair. I said: 'Miss Beaumont, I goofed when I left those Syrettes in the Cadillac. We've got to knock him out; if he makes another noise like that, we'll have the law back here, and this time we won't be able to fool them.'

'How about if I phoned a local doctor while you — ' She got that far, and then answered her own question. 'No. There wouldn't be more than one doctor in a town this size, and he'd be the one they called for the girl, and he'd be sure to connect things.'

For all my experience, I'd been a fool; now I corrected it with a quiet thanks to my luck. I went and got my gun and shoulder holster out of my bag, shucked out of my coat and put my harness back on.

Miss Beaumont said: 'Now we have all the answers. We shoot our way out.'

'We keep our gun on before junior there shoots himself with it.'

She swallowed and turned away. I kept my eye on Ralph. He was still shaking, but his wind was coming back, bringing color to his scrawny cheeks. I said: 'Ralph, let out another yelp and I'll knock you cold, so help me.'

He said: 'Let me kill myself, Andy. Please kill me.'

Miss Beaumont let out a gasp. I asked her: 'He ever do that before, ever say that?'

She shook her head. Her eyes were very

wide. She said: 'No. You put the idea in his head.' But her voice was weak and uncertain. With a little fire, she said: 'I know what you're thinking. You think he's got an — an unbearable burden of guilt.'

'You took the words right out of my mouth. I always talk that way.'

'Oh, don't be the professional hard man. Not now. Not here. I couldn't stand it.'

The boy on the bed was looking from one to the other of us as we spoke, his eyes filled with as much fear as I'd seen in my long years of crime and misery. Patrolling in West Germany once, I'd hauled in a half-grown kid who'd killed one of our men for his boots, and he hadn't looked any more scared than Ralph did then.

The time had come. We couldn't operate on guesses and schoolbook theories anymore. I got my hands ready to choke him off if he got loud, and asked: 'Did you beat up a girl earlier this evening? An Indian girl?'

No matter what anybody tells you, you can't tell when a suspect is lying by reading his face; but we keep on trying. My eyeballs ached with intensity as I waited for Ralph's answer.

He swallowed, forced his eyelids closed, and ran his hands through his hair, trying without success to smooth it. He said: 'Yes, I did. We met outside. I was going to show her how to tell time by the stars, and she said something I didn't like and I hit her.'

'What then?' He didn't answer me at once and I repeated it, my voice as hard as I could make it. Out of the corner of my eye, I could see Miss Beaumont raise her hand as though to stop me. 'What then, Ralph? What did you do then?'

He swallowed again and said clearly: 'Why, she fell down, and I decided that parties weren't so much fun after all, so I walked back here to sleep.'

Miss Beaumont cried: 'Parties. Oh, parties! Hadn't you ever been to one before?'

'Not to a kid's party,' he said. 'Sometimes my father entertains people.'

Miss Beaumont started to cry quietly. Ralph looked at her like she was something under a microscope.

I said: 'Keep it coming, boy. Where did you hit her, so hard that she fell down?'

'In the mouth,' he said. 'Right in the teeth.'

'Once?'

'Why, she wasn't a very big girl. Could I have a glass of water? I'm awfully thirsty.' He was dead calm now, as though telling all this had relieved him.

Miss Beaumont went for the bathroom, and I heard the water start running. I reached down and took both of Ralph's hands in mine, turning them over. There wasn't a mark on them, except the mark of dirt; they were filthy. I let them go.

Tons of weight fell off my back. He hadn't touched the girl! When you hit someone in the mouth hard enough that they have to be sirened to a hospital, you get tooth-marks on your knuckles.

I said: 'Listen, Ralph. Listen, kid, like you never listened before. You haven't done anything. You saw something, and you're — nervous, you know that, it's why we're taking you to the hospital — and you got it all mixed up in your mind. *You didn't hit that girl!'*

Miss Beaumont was back with the water, with the big question in her eyes. 'I'm not kidding,' I said. 'If he'd done it the way he said, his hands would be marked up. They're not.'

Ralph looked from one to the other of us silently. His eyes had the deep glow of a trapped rabbit's.

Miss Beaumont said: 'But why would anyone — '

Telling it in front of Ralph didn't seem wise, but she had the education. 'He saw something he didn't like, did something he's ashamed of. I've had guys confess to crimes before because they thought they'd be safer in a cell. Safer from people, safer from ideas, safer from the lousy world.'

Ralph said: 'I fainted. Like a coward.'

I nodded my wise, uneducated head. 'You see?'

Miss Beaumont gave me the old look that makes a guy feel ninety feet tall, and then she was against me, kissing my cheek. Some of the water she'd brought for Ralph spilled on my coat.

'Easy,' I said, too low — I hoped — for Ralph to hear. 'He hates feminine demonstrations, in himself or anyone else. He nearly passed out at the sight of that dame in her underwear. He — '

Miss Beaumont cut me off, saying, 'Okay, professor,' and turned to Ralph, holding out the pill and the water. But old Doc Bastian was right; he'd fainted again.

And then somebody knocked on the door. I waved her to keep quiet and tend to Ralph. I figured it was Nilsen, or some other law, come back. Now, more than ever, I didn't want them bothering Ralph, making him worse than he was.

But when I opened the door, it wasn't the badges; it was hard guy Morgan from cabin Number 11. The woman stood behind him, but she'd put on a dress and shoes now. She hadn't combed her hair, though.

Morgan said: 'What's going on in here? We wanta know what you're doin' to that kid you dragged in here!'

I said a single, simple four-letter word and let him have it, right in his thin-lipped mouth. He went staggering back and down. I said: 'Lady, drag him to your den, or leave him there. But it's about time this motel quieted down.' Then I shut the door, turned to Miss Beaumont and held out my fist.

'See?' She looked, and she saw all right; the knuckles were barked on his teeth.

I went in the bathroom to use soap on the little scratches, and she went next door and came back holding a pill bottle. She said: 'Sleeping pills. Mine, not Ralph's. What do you think?'

'Soon as he comes to, I'll give him a dose. And when the Cad gets here, I think I'll knock him out with morphine and break a few state laws getting to Kansas. Whatever the hell happened up the hill at the party, it isn't our fault; let's just get out of here.'

She said: 'Good night then, Andy. And I think you're wonderful.'

'I'll look outside and see if those drips have gone back to their love nest.'

She tilted her head up and said: 'Oh, give them a minute or so. I'm in no hurry.'

So I kissed her. Hell, I'm a public

servant, and I presume she paid taxes; and it was what she wanted.

Well, it was easy duty.

11

The rest of that night was a cinch. Ralph came out of his faint, and before he could start arguing, I gave him two of the sleeping pills; the label said one to three, and I played it safe. They started working at once; he mumbled for a while, some stuff about the stars and the Big Dipper swinging around Stella Polaris, and some stuff about Indians and the Bering Strait, and then he went to sleep.

I pulled his shoes and his pants off and rolled him under the covers, and got a washrag and cleaned up his hands and his tear-stained face. I'd drunk two glasses of water, and started to get ready for bed when I heard a car start up.

Cop's curiosity dragged me out; it was the maroon Buick. It turned in the arch and went away to the east, towards New Mexico. I counted three heads as a truck's headlights glared on the Buick's windshield. So they were all gone, and if I hadn't been so tired, I'd have waved them bye-bye.

Instead I went to bed. Maybe sometime I'd been more tired, but I couldn't remember when. My hand felt for the gun under my pillow, my fingers checked the safety catch to make sure it was on, and I was asleep.

Next thing I knew, light was coming through the slats in the venetian blinds, and my watch said quarter to eight. I rolled my feet to the floor and looked at the other bed. Ralph was still asleep, but his bedclothes were all churned up; he'd been riding the old nightmare.

I shaved and washed with the bathroom door open in case he came out of it, but when I was all dressed he was still asleep. I took his pulse, worrying because I'd given him sleeping pills on someone else's prescription, but all I learned was that he had a pulse.

Female voices outside caused me to crack the venetian blind and peer out. Miss Beaumont, neat and impersonal in her traveling suit, was talking to Elizabeth of Somewater in front of their room. I went out.

'Elizabeth's on her way,' Miss Beaumont said. 'She's leaving the Hudson for her father.'

'How about some breakfast first?'

Elizabeth shook her round head. 'Lots of the town kids eat at the coffee pot next to the school. I've never done that. Boy, there'll be winging and dinging this morning. Yak, yaketty, yak, yak.' Then a shadow crossed her face. 'It's awful, and I know it — but boy, when you get to sleep in town one night in your life, isn't it something that it's a hot time like this!'

Mr. Bartlett's money was still holding out. I folded a five with the fingers of one hand and slapped it into her palm. 'We owe you breakfast.'

But she looked at it. 'It's too much.'

'We put you to a lot of trouble.'

'Well, all right . . . and thanks a load.' She skipped to the old Hudson, dragged some books off the floor, and carried them out of the motel yard in what would have been a dead run if she'd been a year younger.

Seen in the hard Arizona morning, Miss Beaumont looked like she'd never

161

been kissed by me or anyone else but her parents. I told her: 'Go get some breakfast, and bring me black coffee and a couple of doughnuts. Ralph's still asleep.'

She flicked a hand at her skirt. 'My nylons are still drying; I forgot to wash them last night. Anyway, breakfast doesn't mean a thing to me, and you look as if you consume horses every morning.'

'Just Shetland ponies.'

'I can watch Ralph just fine. He thinks of me as some kind of nurse, anyway.'

So I walked up to the coffee shop. It was open, but the clock on the wall said it was just seven o'clock; we'd moved into Mountain Time. I sat down at the counter and ordered the Number 4 breakfast: orange juice, oatmeal, a breakfast steak and one egg, buttered toast and coffee. Miss Beaumont had sized me up right.

I was mopping up egg yolk with a forkful of steak when State Highway Patrolman Nilsen came and sat down next to me. He'd shaved someplace or other, but that didn't hide the fact that he'd had no sleep. 'Mornin' Bastian.'

'Hi, Nilsen. Let my expense account

buy your breakfast.'

'Sometime you gotta tell me how you get jobs like yours.' He signaled the counter woman, who seemed to know what he ate; she didn't come near us but said something through the pass-through to the cook.

'Getting anyplace, Nils?'

He shook his head sourly and drained a glass of ice water. 'I musta smoked two packs of cigarettes through the night. Naw, noplace. Gruder and the rest of the county, plus some dudes from the county seat — you know, sheriff's posse with saddles and horses that'd cost a real cop a year's pay — are out riding around in the hills.'

The woman brought him tomato juice. He fingered up a piece of ice, and chewed on it. 'One thing,' he said. 'Nowadays when a posseman falls off his horse, they send a helicopter; we don't have to get him out with a stretcher.'

'Got any solid ideas?'

'Why, yeah. I thought you'd a figured it out, too, a guy with the experience to get a gover'ment job like you got.'

'Don't take it out on me, pal. I've gone without sleep in my time.'

He said: 'Sure, sure, sorry,' and brightened a little when he got a coffee pot and a cup. All I'd gotten was the cup. 'Highway job,' Nilsen said, pouring the steamy black into his cup.

'Oh?'

'You get that in your Naranjo Vista too, or is that job just cover?'

'Naranjo Vista's real enough,' I said. 'But I'm a reserve major in the army, cleared for C.I.D. work.' Which was true. 'No, our town isn't on a highway. There's a freeway about five miles away, but that's different.'

'You're damn well right. Patrolling a freeway is like getting paid to test mattresses. But these open highways, this 66 — wow. Every punk and no-good and petty hood's out on 66, hitchhiking or maybe pushing an old jalopy, no money, no gas card; these little towns look wide open to them, and God knows they are; a state cruiser goes through every couple of hours, sticking to 66, and sometimes a deputy like Gruder looks over the back streets.'

'Driving 66, you'd never know there were any back streets.'

'The punks know.' He got his ham and eggs then, and plain toast, which he started buttering with ice-hard butter; I hate toast that way, but he seemed to savor it. Around a mouthful of it, he said: 'How come you left your people?'

'The boy's still asleep, the woman's pretty competent, and it's daylight. From here I can see if anybody drives in, but they're not likely to.'

He said: 'Yeah,' without interest. He was a fast eater; we finished even, and I grabbed his check. He said: 'Well, thanks. We get per diem if we work more than twelve hours in a day, but it's a flat rate.'

'Think you'll get whoever did the job?'

He stood up, stretching, all his leather creaking, and flipped out a package of cigarettes. I took one, and we blew smoke at each other while he said: 'Aw, we might. We've got some of the California boys watching the inspection shed on their side; we got our own men, and New Mexico's alerted. If money's taken, we usually get them, they get big with their

165

dough in some highway bar. But in this one — I dunno, unless it's a screwball. More likely a hot hood, and the girl wandered out of the party and saw him trying to make a house across the street.'

We strolled outside, and he said: 'Want I should get on the horn and see how your car's coming?'

'Be nice of you.'

'Professional courtesy,' he said. 'But I was just a sergeant in the marines, so I suppose I couldn't get some of these extra-pay federal jobs?' It was a big question mark that hung in the air between us while he reached into his cruiser and warmed the radio, unhooked the mike and put out a call letter.

The cruiser over west answered, and Nilsen said: 'Wanta find out if that Cad at Somewater'll be fixed? The driver's a friend of mine.'

The other patrolman flashed call letters back and then: 'Ham Gotch was out with his head under the front wheels last time I went by.'

Nilsen raised an eyebrow at me, and I said: 'Then he's got the part.'

Nilsen said: 'Thanks and over and out,' and switched off. 'You oughta be outa here by noon, Andy.'

But I was worried. They're my people, it's my business, but in case you don't know: look out for policemen when they get too nice. A life spent with drunks, crooks, killers and thieves doesn't make for a generous nature.

So I tried something. 'A job with the C.I.D. wouldn't be possible, Nil. Anyway, the amount of active duty I get doesn't come to a hell of a lot in a year. But if and when you retire from the Arizona Highway Patrol — '

He cut in, almost eagerly: 'Less than two years from now I get eligible for a pension.'

'I could do something for you in one of the California subdivisions. I'll be chief of one of them by then. You have my address in your book.'

He nodded, standing there in the morning sun, squinting at me to see if I meant it. I stared back, trying to make him out. It looked like all he wanted was a job that, added to his half pay or two thirds pay or whatever it was in Arizona, would leave him sitting pretty. Or read another way, he was just pumping me.

Finally he said: 'That'd be all right.' He reached inside the car, got his notebook out of its clip, wrote on a back page and tore it out for me. 'That's my home address. Lemme know when you get back. What'd it be?'

'Probably desk officer. A man can't slug the highways forever.'

He said: 'Sure. Well, take care of your traveling circus,' and got into his car and turned the switch.

I walked back to our rooms slowly. We had an hour or so till we got the Cadillac back, then we had about three hundred miles of Arizona after that, and it was heavy on me; too much time and mileage. My conscience was clear, sure; I knew Ralph hadn't done anything he shouldn't, but I was nervous about him being questioned as though it was me that had the raw nerves inside.

He woke up at nine, Arizona time, and I walked him up to the coffee shop while he chowed. 'Can I go swimming after breakfast?' he asked.

'Our car ought to be back soon.'

'Well, golly, I should think I could take time out to take a dip. Gosh, I never seem to be having any fun, and there's a winging old pool back there . . . '

With great relief I said: 'Here's the car now.'

He looked out the window and said: 'Yes, that's Father's car. You'd better look under it and make sure he got the tie-rod end. If he tries to charge you for a whole new tie rod, don't you pay him.'

'You look under and see what's new.' I shoved money at the waitress, and we got out of there. Five minutes, I was thinking; five minutes to pay the man and throw our bags in the oar. Mine was all packed and ready, and I was willing to bet large money that Miss Beaumont's was, too. Ralph could pack when he got through looking at the car. It was a matter of keeping him busy until he was on his way. Maybe I could sneak up on him and push a Syrette into his arm when he wasn't looking.

Now we were walking back towards our room. What kind of a person was he under the amazing learning, the startling memory, the alarming neurosis? Last night he had thought he'd assaulted a girl, and this morning he was miserable because I wouldn't let him swim, and in between times he was lost in a book.

Too much for a simple cop. There was the man from Somewater talking to Miss Beaumont, leaning on the Cadillac. The trunk was open and our bags were already in. She said: 'We're ready to go. I left your book out of your bag, Ralph.'

'That paperback? I'd rather have one of my own books, but I suppose that would be too much trouble.'

I walked to the back of the Cad and slammed the trunk lid down. 'Yes, it would be.'

Miss Beaumont was looking at me like worms were crawling out of my nose. I made an effort to remember a name and said: 'Mr. Gotch, how much do I owe you?'

'I got a bill right here. Hope Lissy behaved herself.'

She hated to be called that, she'd said. The bill was for twenty-five bucks, seven-fifty for the part, about eight dollars for phone calls and only ten dollars for his own labor. It wasn't enough, but I didn't have time to throw any of Mr. Bartlett's money around just then. I waved away the five dollars in change he tried to give me and gestured to Miss Beaumont to get Ralph into the car. But he had to sign a receipt. This involved getting out a stub of pencil, wetting it — what does that do for a pencil, anyway? — on his tongue, and scrawling a name, and the word *Paid*. Then he said: 'What's the date, anyway?'

'Don't bother,' I said.

He looked worried. 'Well, okay. Say, my brother-in-law said they had some excitement here, at a kid's party.'

'Yeah.' Let him find out Elizabeth had been there. Or not. I was saying good-bye to Cupra.

'These towns are no place to bring up kids,' he said. 'Give me the country, every time.'

Sure, I thought. *You're lost without your windmill to help you think*. I pumped his hand very hard, said a couple of thank-yous, and got behind the wheel. Ralph was already slumped against the right-hand door, scowling at the paperback *The Meaning of Art* that we'd bought last night. Miss Beaumont sat between us, very straight, her now-dry nylons neatly crossed on the hump the transmission made in the floor, her eyes half-closed. I imagine she was praying, if professional psychologists are allowed to have any religion.

The Cad moved out easily, I turned right at the arch, and we were back on 66. Fifty-five seconds later, the last house of Cupra was behind us, and I let the speed build up.

12

Highway 66 really climbed, though not enough to bother a Cadillac. I found I was seeing the country with a new eye; there were a lot more towns on the road than I had ever dreamed of. Ralph's and Elizabeth's eyes were mine now; riding this way, he would be seeing groups of unpoliced streets, while she'd be seeing metropolitan pleasures.

My companions were not talkative. Ralph was mad about the swim, and Miss Beaumont, I suppose, about the rude way I'd answered Ralph. We crossed into a new county, and out of Gruder's jurisdiction; but he was off in the mountains, hunting imaginary badmen. I wished him luck. He'd have to be awfully polite, with all those amateur posse-men along, and him wanting to be sheriff next election.

We went through Seligman, and I hoped that Cupra's football team would overcome the boys of that sprawling city of less than a thousand inhabitants.

Arizona roads have milestones that indicate how far you are from the California border. As we headed into Flagstaff, we passed one that said 225; I asked Miss Beaumont to get the map out of the glove compartment and see how far to New Mexico.

The compartment, of course, was locked; but the car was one of those that will run without an ignition key, once it's started. She took the key and got the map out, frowning a little. There was a map there, and she bent over it; for all her brilliance, she was not at home with a road map.

'Less than a hundred and ninety,' she said.

I had slowed down for Flagstaff; we were running alongside the railroad. This was high mountain country, lumber country; the smoke from a sawmill's sawdust burner shone thick against the mountain sky. It was about noon, but there was a bite under the sunny air.

'Good,' I said. 'Gallup's the first town in New Mexico, isn't it? We'll eat there.'

'Golly,' Ralph said. 'I don't know what

you've got against Arizona.' He jerked a thumb out the window. 'It'd be fun to stop here, or we could have stopped back at Williams, where all those Indian-goods stores are. This is kind of a dumb trip, just balling the jack across 66, never stopping to see anything.' He took the map from Miss Beaumont, opened it, and scowled. 'We pass all kinds of winging stuff. Walnut Canyon, that's cliff dwellings, and the big meteor crater, and the Petrified Forest. Gosh, I want to see something. There's all kinds of places to eat along the way, and we could do a little sightseeing. How about it, Miss Beaumont?'

'We'd better keep going,' she said.

'Golly Moses, old people are dopes,' Ralph said, and slammed the map shut, forcing it against its natural creases. The key was still in the glove compartment lock; before Miss Beaumont could do anything, he had the compartment open and had found the two Syrettes of morphine that the honest state police had left there.

'Hey, looky there . . . ' He had the box out and open. The sterile needles glittered in the sun. We were out of Flagstaff a bit, passing the turnoff to Walnut Canyon, but he'd forgotten about sightseeing. He picked one of the Syrettes out of its cotton nest and read the label. 'Hey, morphine. It's against the law — ' He put it back, shut the box, and twisted his long legs around so he could stare at us. 'You a dope fiend or something, Andy?'

I kept my hands on the wheel and my focus straight ahead, but I'm good at seeing out of the side of my eye. He was pale and worried, and wild-looking again. You could never tell what he was going to do. He said, blurting it out, his voice blurry as a three-year-old kid's: 'You're gonna do something to me. You're gonna stick those needles in me, an' do somethin'.'

'No, Ralph, no.' That was me. Miss Beaumont just look distressed. I got a firm grip on the wheel; he was capable of lunging across and trying to steer us into a ditch.

But instead, he grabbed the outside door handle and tried to open it. I twisted the car sharply, throwing him against

Miss Beaumont, crushing her against me. The door didn't open; a good thing, since we were going close to seventy.

My official voice barked: 'Break it up, Ralph! You're being a damn fool!'

Sometimes things work; I got through to him, and he let go of the handle. Miss Beaumont, I saw, was tugging at his arm with both her hands and getting nowhere.

Suddenly he heaved the little box out of the window. I cut a glance over, and it flew open in midair, flash of needle and glass, and I was reasonably sure the Syrettes would break when they hit.

'There,' he said, 'that will show you!'

Gone was the scholar who could tell you what wood grew in Spain, how a two-way radio was made, what was on the other side of the moon. He was just a slightly spoiled, sulky kid now. But this wasn't insanity, it was just adolescence, the sudden swing from maturity to childishness and back again. That thought came into my head unbidden, and it would go out again.

The time had come to talk; our pet psychologist was dumb as a giraffe. I said:

'That's great, kid. I'm a cop, did you forget? If we run into an accident, traffic trouble, I'm expected to do something. That was an important part of my first-aid equipment.'

'Hey,' he said. 'Hey, that's something.'

He said the last word clearly, against his mumbling it before. I couldn't tell if his temper was over, or if he'd gone into a different phase. I wished to God Miss Beaumont would take over.

'Well,' I said, 'forget it.' About as brilliant a speech as a halfwit ever made.

He said: 'Awww . . . ' dragging it out in melancholy apology, and then he started to cry. And so, heaven help me, did Miss Beaumont.

Ahead, a huge sign signaled the turnoff to the Meteor Crater. It was a dirt road, and I looked up it quickly: no dust clouds. The tourists were probably all eating lunch. I turned up there. There'd be water and maybe solitude, and a chance to stretch our legs and move around a little and get our egos back into adjustment.

The road was about a ten-minute run at half speed. We were stopped once while

I paid a fee to an indifferent-looking clerk; Miss Beaumont and Ralph kept quiet, their heads turned away from the booth. Then on to the edge of the meteor. I parked and locked the car, and got the keys back in my pocket. I was lucky; Ralph hadn't thought to go through the glove compartment to see if there really was the rest of a first-aid kit there. There wasn't.

A little shack with a platform and some dime-telescopes overlooked the meteor. A loudspeaker was giving a spiel about the meteor — or the crater, I should say, because the spiel said you couldn't see the meteor, but test borings had located it underground. It was made of nickel and iron, with a little platinum and even some diamonds.

'Hey,' Ralph said, 'golly, that's something. Diamonds, huh? There's some meteors in the American Museum of Natural History in New York, they're mostly nickel, but no diamonds. Hey, did you ever hear about the meteor that fell in Russia a long time ago, about fifty years, and set fire — '

He was off. Or maybe I should say he was on again; he was completely the likable, learned prodigy. He rambled on; Miss Beaumont wandered away to the drinking fountain in front of the shack that housed the loudspeaker. She drank, and rubbed cold water on her face, and used her handkerchief and lipstick. There were circles of strain under her eyes that hadn't been there when we'd started the day.

Ralph was completely happy, though. He had an amazing capacity for forgetting the shocking scenes he created from time to time.

There was the necessity to revise my plans. Much as I wanted to hurry out of Arizona, much as I wanted to shove the rest of 66 behind me and turn north for Kansas, speed seemed inadvisable. Letting Ralph out of the car every so often to do a little sightseeing and acquire a little knowledge — or air knowledge he already had — seemed necessary. Well, it would be no worse than traveling with a puppy or a child. All young things need to stretch their legs and kick up their heels from time to time.

We got back in the Cadillac and headed for the highway. We turned east again and ran the road; went through Winslow while Ralph read his *Meaning of Art*; ran some more at top speed and slowed down for Joseph City or Joseph's City, an eastern-looking little town. Ralph threw his book in the back seat, finished with it, and explained how Mormons had founded this town. He gave a short discourse on Mormon architecture, past and present, and we went on some more, and into Holbrook, less than seventy-five miles from the state line.

I was trying to remember if New Mexico had agricultural inspection, like Arizona and California. Two or three years had passed since I'd been there; and I supposed sometimes they did, sometimes they didn't.

On the north, the Painted Desert came up; but it was too near noon, Ralph said, for it to look like much; you need shadows. Still, he favored us with a rundown on what minerals caused the different colors; green for copper and red for iron, and so on.

Miss Beaumont nudged me. I glanced over, and her hands were in her lap, with one thumb at a queer angle; she was pointing in a quiet and ladylike way. I followed her direction. Ralph's hands were twitching, his legs crossing and uncrossing. He was getting pent up and nervous again. I said: 'Want to take a gander at the Petrified Forest?'

His voice came at me sharp and a little cracked, like a kid's whose is changing. 'Thought you were in an all-fired winging hurry, Lieutenant.' He hadn't called me by my title since yesterday.

'We don't have to be all that winging,' I said. I was watching his hands; they had stopped twitching and were still, but curved claw-like, as though they were about to pounce. 'What is it they say? Live a little.'

Ralph said uncertainly: 'Well, if you don't mind, it's occurred to me that we should find just the same colorations in the petrified wood as you do in the Painted Desert. Do you know what makes wood petrify?'

For once he'd hit on something I did know — Lord knew from where — but I hid my little kernel of learning and said: 'No, tell me.'

He did, at some length and with enough detail to convince me I really hadn't known at all; I just thought I had. Under cover of his talk, Miss Beaumont reached over and patted my thigh, and I glowed with the feeling of something done right for once.

A sign said we were passing from Apache to Navajo County, and then I had to slow down for the entrance to the National Monument. One of those flat-hatted kids with a ranger's badge collected a fee and gave us a one-day pass, and we were in the Petrified Forest. We elected to park the car and walk through what the ranger said was the Black Forest; we helped ourselves to a folder at the museum.

The trail was steep and rough, and after a moment Miss Beaumont said she thought she'd turn back and wait for us in the museum.

Properly speaking, where we were wasn't petrified forest at all. But Ralph had forgotten all about his research; he scrambled around the rugged country, climbing on rocks and jumping off them, and had himself a time. I kept as close to him as possible.

He came back to me after a while and sat down on a rock, hard. 'Boy, that was fun.'

'Have yourself a winging time?' I asked.

He looked up at me, and suddenly shot out his bony hand and caught mine, giving it a squeeze. 'You're a nice guy, Andy. You know, I like you!'

Praise from a screwball shouldn't make a hard-boiled cop happy, but suddenly it did; I felt like the time fifteen years before when a colonel had pinned gold bars on my shoulders and I'd stopped being an enlisted man.

'You're all right yourself, Ralph,' I said. 'Though somewhat smarter than most of my friends.'

He laughed. 'I just have a good memory, is all.' Then something went wrong inside his head. His fingers crooked and he ran them up over his face and into his hair.

I dropped down to my knees and got an arm over his shoulder. 'Something wrong, boy? If there is, you got a friend, you know.'

He said in a voice that cut through me: 'There's nothing a friend can do about it,' and started crying again, but very quietly, like a grown man, a sound that would break your heart.

My arm came away from his shoulders. I was tampering with something I didn't know anything about. He'd gone completely to pieces yesterday when Miss Beaumont had offered him a little motherly sympathy; maybe fatherly sympathy was as bad. Back in that first war I'd enlisted in, plenty of guys had married at nineteen; if I'd done that I could have had a son his age.

How would I have felt if I'd done that, and he'd turned out like this: brainy, likable, and completely screw-loose? I wasn't used to examining my emotions; I dropped it.

He looked up and mopped at his face with a dirty handkerchief. 'I'm sorry.'

'This sun's pretty hot, and you've been running around without a hat.'

'Sure. The sun's pretty hot, all right.'

He got up and we walked slowly back up the bad path; at times it was too narrow for both of us, and I dropped back.

13

Miss Beaumont was waiting for us at the monument museum, sitting on a bench on the flagstone court. 'Learn anything, men?'

'Yeah.' That was me, while Ralph headed for the water cooler. 'Learned that Arizona isn't flat.'

Ralph came away from the water; he'd soaked some in his hair and was trying to straighten that wild mass with his fingers. I handed him my pocket comb and took a drink myself; it was cold enough to make my teeth ache. Ralph said: 'If you've never seen the museum, it's pretty beautiful.'

Lying, I said: 'I've seen it.'

'Well, so have I.'

So we trooped back to the Cadillac. Ralph held the door politely for Miss Beaumont, the first time he'd done that, and then got in, shut the door, and put his head back on the seat. Before I could get us into transit, he was asleep, his mouth a little open, his young teeth gleaming in the hot sun. I turned the air conditioner up a notch.

Miss Beaumont said: 'What — ' but then we were at the check station, where we'd bought our pass.

I slowed down and the ranger waved me on, saying something. I stopped the car and said: 'What was that?'

He had a bad Texas drawl, somewhat cleaned up by somebody's college. 'I just said, hurry back. Did your friends find you?'

'What friends?'

'Ah, that's too bad,' the ranger said. 'I told them to look in both parking lots, but people overlook the no'th one. They stayed such a sho't time, I figured they'd run right into you.'

'No, they didn't.' I could hear my own voice, cold as death.

'Well if y'all are headin' east, you'll prob'ly catch them. That red Buick of theirs is no fittin' match for a Cadillac.'

'Oh,' I said, 'a maroon Buick. Two men and a woman?'

'Three men and a woman.'

'Them,' I said idiotically. 'We've got a date to all stop together tonight. We'll find them.'

'Fine,' he said. And then: 'Hurry back,' and crossed to the other side to check a tourist car in.

I got onto the highway, drove slowly around the first bend, and stopped. My knees were shaking as they took my weight; but that doesn't mean a thing. They always have shaken before action. But they've never failed to take me to where I had to go. Lots of times I thought they were going to twist and run away, but they never have.

Miss Beaumont slid out of the car on my side and stood beside me. 'What is it?'

Traffic roared and whistled by in both directions. The sun brought sweat out in my hair, and promptly dried it. I said: 'Those drips. They really are following us.'

'The one you hit?'

'The one I hit, the one I pulled out of the swimming pool, and now there's a new one. And the woman, the woman with a face like an unbaked raisin cake.'

Miss Beaumont squinted up at the Arizona sun. 'That's a very picturesque remark, but it doesn't get us anywhere. Why in the world would they follow us?'

By then I was on my knees looking under the car. What I saw was the underside of a car. I said: 'I wish I'd gone to Motor Maintenance School instead of MPs. We'll have to wake the kid up.'

'No, Andy, no.'

I stood up and brushed at my knees. 'I know what you mean. But — I don't think now that our tie rod broke by accident. I'm scared to drive this thing if they got to it in the parking lot back there.'

She nodded. 'I can see that. But I wasn't away from the car very long. Just to look at the polished stones in the museum.' Her smile was a masterpiece of unhappiness. 'I didn't study the geological charts.' She did her two-handed grab of my arm. 'Andy — if you drove very slowly?'

The map of Arizona unrolled in my head again. Thirty, thirty-one miles to the junction with the road that went down

190

into the Apache country, to towns like St. John, Springerville, Show Low . . . there'd be a settlement of some sort at the junction. There might even be one before that, something with a grease rack and a man who knew what the bottom of a Cadillac ought to look like.

'We'll take a chance.'

Ralph slept as I slid the car into drive, taking off like the drive shaft was made of glass. Miss Beaumont sat up between us as though she was made of crystal, waiting for Caruso to sing a high note.

A couple of minutes later, a sign said there was gas ahead. But on those high desert roads, 'ahead' could mean two miles or ten. I made the Cadillac do its snail crawl.

But the gas place we came to in about five miles — or fifteen minutes — was no Somewater. It was a curio joint with a snake pit — See Deadly Monsters — a single pump selling low-test gas, a counter for cold pop and greasy hamburgers. There was no use stopping there.

Prayer is not usual to me, but I prayed that Ralph wouldn't wake up. If I'd had the morphine, this would have been a prime time to use it. We couldn't answer any questions he asked without making him nervous, and that was not what we were there to do. And he'd be sure to ask questions about our snail-pacing.

Another gas sign, another curio shop; it featured live Jack rabbits. 66 is a slum of a highway these days.

Finally we found one, a grease rack, modern pumps, a sign that said a mechanic was on twenty-four-hour duty. It was a big town, too, maybe two hundred people. But Elizabeth had stopped me laughing at towns that size.

I turned in, and as I stopped the Cad, Ralph woke up. 'What's wrong?' His voice was muzzy with sleep.

'There's a funny squeak in one of the front wheels,' I said, letting my breath out.

Ralph said: 'Ah-ha. I'll bet Elizabeth's father didn't have the right kind of grease for a tie-rod end. The bearings — '

Miss Beaumont cut him off. 'Before we leave Arizona, Ralph, I'd like to buy a piece of turquoise jewelry. I'll bet you could keep me from being cheated.'

He said: 'Oh, yes, it's easy to tell real turquoise. It's supposed to have a waxy feel, with a hardness of six and a blue streak. But they have turquoise jewelry in New Mexico, too. The Zuñis do wonderful inlay work, and really Gallup is just about the center of Navajo activity, though their tribal headquarters is in — '

She was leading him away, saying something about wanting a souvenir of Arizona, which might have made me laugh, if there had been a laugh left in me.

A gangly guy in an old-fashioned coat sweater ambled out of the filling station. 'Gas, mister?'

'You the mechanic?'

'No, he's out on a call. He ought to be back any minute; it was just to start Mr. Ranklen's car, and Mr. Ranklen usually leaves his ignition on, is all.'

'There's a funny noise in my Cad. I'd like him to look at it.'

This was a real joker. 'You can't look at a noise. How's about if I run it up on the rack? It probably just needs grease.'

'Fine, but I'd like your mechanic to look it over.'

He shrugged and turned away, then stood in front of the rack signaling me till he got me lined up. I drove onto the rack and we both stood looking stupid till it went up into the air. He tried to whirl the wheels, and when they wouldn't whirl, he reached up and in and released the emergency brake. His hands were greasy; I made a note to wipe the brake handle before I drove again. Then he prowled around under the car, turning wheels, tapping things, whistling between his teeth in a high-pitched note that was hard to listen to. It broke off as a truck slammed to a stop in front of the place, the chains on the rear hoist clanging. I went outside.

The mechanic was little more prepossessing than his helper. He said: 'Do something for you, Mac?'

'Look over the Cad. It's making a noise in the front end.'

He shrugged. 'Probably just needs a grease job.'

'But I want a mechanic to look at it.'

He rubbed his hands together. 'Listen, I can look at your car. But looking at a Cadillac, now, it would cost you ten dollars. Whether I find anything or not.'

'Well, people don't live on Highway 66 for their health.'

He gave me a dirty look, then shrugged and said: 'If you're driving a Cad, you're probably good for ten bucks,' and went out to his truck. He came back with a flashlight, joined his pal under the car, and went through the same routine of whirling wheels and tapping things, using the handle of a wrench he got out of his hip pocket.

Miss Beaumont and Ralph had disappeared into a 'trading post' down the road. It might have been one, for all I know. We were just below the big Navajo reservation, but I didn't see any Indians around. Now they came out, and went into a combined café and shop next door.

The boss of the grease rack came out to join me, wiping his hands on a piece of gunnysack, and sighing as though exhausted. 'Nothing wrong with your car, Mac. It's the tires.'

'Tires?'

He nodded. Tears seemed to be forming in both his eyes. 'Shot, Mac. You might make Gallup on them, if you drove mighty, mighty easy.' I had never heard such a sad voice. 'That is, if you let me sell you a replacement for that right front. *It* wouldn't take you to that chile joint down the road.'

'Tires, huh?' This was my day for sparkling conversation.

'Lemme show you, Mac.' He bent over. 'Truth is, you can't trust no one these days. The big manufacturers, they put *seconds* on the new cars. Even *thirds*. No regard for human life. Now, when a customer drives out of my place, Mac, I want to be sure he's going to live, not end up in a ditch from a blowout. Lemme show you.'

Fascinated, I followed him back to where the Cadillac sprawled indignantly overhead. He turned a rear tire dexterously. 'See those little cracks?' I barely could; they were hairline-thin, paper-deep. 'Pretty soon they all join into one big crack and — blooey!'

'I'll take a chance,' I said.

His sadness became despair. 'If you got no consideration for your own life, Mac, think of the poor cops who'll have to haul you out of the ditch. Bloody. Broken up. With maybe your head through the windshield.'

I hadn't had much fun the last day or so; I had some now. I took out my wallet with the blue and gold Naranjo Vista badge pinned in plain sight, then produced my federal clearance card and let him look at it. I took my notebook off the other hip, and a pencil from my inside jacket pocket; I flipped the jacket slowly so he could see the gun. Writing down the name of the place off its gas company sign, I said: 'You own this station?'

'No, Officer, I don't.' I was no longer Mac. 'I'm just running it while the owner's away. He promised me a commission on tires.'

My head nodded wisely. 'I wondered. These tires were government-checked five hundred miles back. If there's anything wrong with them, it'll be a court-martial for the man who put them on. You'll make a good witness. I can see you know your business.'

His teary voice was brisk and cheerful. 'Officer, I don't know a thing about tires.

I'm a car mechanic. I'll tell you. There's a big gov'ment installation other side of Gallup. Fort Wingate. Have someone there look at them. I could be making a mistake.'

'Could be.' I snapped the notebook shut, put it on my left hip, and got my wallet off my right. 'Ten bucks for an inspection, right?'

'Mister, I didn't do nothing but look.'

'You said ten dollars, you get ten dollars.' I held it out to him.

His fingers twitched. The greasy sacking fell to the ground. 'What do I sign?'

'Nothing. This goes under mileage and incidentals.'

He took the ten, then released the pressure in the hoist and the car came down. I got a paper towel from his gas pump and wiped the brake handle where his assistant had touched it. We could have used gas, but he would have expected a government form to sign. I asked him: 'You went over the running gear. Is it all right?'

'Honest to God, mister, I'm a good mechanic.'

So I'd spent time on a false alarm.

Maybe it was all coincidence; maybe one of the mush-heads had wanted to thank me for pulling him out of the pool; maybe the other one had brought a friend along to revenge the punch in the jaw I'd given him; maybe they wanted to sell us some bad oil stock; or maybe Miss Beaumont had scared them off. Though cracking a tie-rod end was just a matter of a blow with a six-pound hammer, I was sure.

But no use crying over spent minutes. I drove the few yards to the café and stopped, and Miss Beaumont and Ralph came out and got in. She was waving one hand to show off a new ring. 'Persian turquoise,' she said.

'Funny souvenir of Arizona.' I was on the highway and rolling.

'The Navajo silverwork and stone cutting's all real,' Ralph said. 'The Indians like to use Persian turquoise for some of their best work. It's a wonderful ring.'

'Ralph bought it,' Miss Beaumont said. 'It's a gift.' I stole a glance from the crowded 66 to her. Her hand was held up proudly, the polished silver and her eyes both shining.

'Father gave me ten dollars for spending money,' Ralph said. 'But there's been nothing to spend it on.'

Which might not have flattered most women getting a gift, but it didn't seem to crush Miss Beaumont.

We rolled on. Signs started to say that this was our last chance to buy Arizona gas. On the other side of the line, of course, there would be signs warning westbound folk of their last chance to buy New Mexico gas. I —

The officer who pulled us down didn't use his siren and red light; 66 was four-lane there. He just came along side and waved, and I pulled to the side.

Miss Beaumont's ringed hand dropped into her lap; my stomach dropped into my hips. I took my foot off the gas and slowly drifted to the side of the road.

The patrolman stopped ahead of me and got out and walked back. He walked like all the cops in the world; slowly and with a roll to accommodate the heavy iron on his hip.

Miss Beaumont had her praying look back on. Ralph looked noncommittal.

14

He took his time. Cars no longer have running boards, so he contented himself with slowly folding his arms, putting them on the windowsill next to me and leaning on them. 'Lieutenant Bastian?'

'Yes.' I didn't dare look at Ralph. If a simple agricultural inspector had sent him high, this should blow him all over the blue Arizona heavens.

'Nilsen radioed me you'd be coming this way,' he said.

'Oh. How's Nil coming with his investigation?' It didn't do any harm to be friendly, even chummy. I had filed away the fact that his fellow officers called him Nil, though Nils came easier to my tongue.

'He's back on patrol,' the officer said. 'The plainclothes division from Tucson have taken over . . . Nil and I used to be partners when we used to ride two to a car.'

'The Dolly Sisters,' I said. I started to get out of the car. The sooner he was removed from Ralph, the better. It looked like just a friendly visit, a professional chat, but never trust a cop is the primary rule — even for other cops.

'Yeah,' he said. 'That's what they used to call us. I'd forgotten that. I'm Jake Withers.'

The first name meant nothing; it could be friendliness, it could be out of a handbook on how to put a suspect at his ease. I couldn't look at Miss Beaumont to warn her to let me handle this.

And then something wonderful came over me; I knew I didn't *have* to look at her. We were in complete accord, for all that most of our talk together seemed to descend to bickering.

But she knew what I knew, and I knew what she knew, except for some of the long words she would have learned in all those colleges. We were a team.

We *both* knew that cops don't stop you for nothing, or because they're lonesome. Cops are always lonesome; it comes with the badge, the oath of office and the gun.

Something in our story still needed checking out, and Jake Withers had stopped us to check it. And we both knew, Miss Beaumont and I, that we couldn't let him question Ralph. Ralph had confessed to assaulting Peggy Sue Cuero once — presumably to cover the unmanly fact of his fainting — and he might do it again. And then we'd be in the bubbling soup. Newspapers would scream that Millionaire's Son Confesses to Assault, headline-hungry officers and political attorneys would descend on us, and Mr. Bartlett's reputation, which he had hired us to protect, would be smashed.

Worse than that — and I knew Miss Beaumont felt as I did about this, too — Ralph would be smashed. She hadn't been with me on the Black Forest trail when he'd cried against my shoulder, and I hadn't been with her when she sat in the white leather chair and let him throw furniture at her; but like a good well-seasoned team, we knew that a cop questioning would groove that kid's nerves past the recovery point, and we had to prevent it. It was why I'd stifled my own curiosity and never asked him what really happened at the slipped-disc party. And our motives were not for the money we were going to be paid, but because we both loved Ralph.

All this went through my head fast, as I stared ahead to where the end of Arizona ought to be, just over the horizon. It was up to me to handle Jake Withers, and it was up to her to keep Ralph quiet, and I had as much confidence that one would be done as the other. It made me feel pretty good.

I was out of the car now, moving slowly ahead to sit on a front fender. Jake Withers moved with me. I held out my hand in such a way that he turned his back on Ralph and Miss Beaumont to take it. 'Nice to know you, Jake.'

'Your first name's Andy, isn't it? Nil said you were talking to him about work in California. I'm due for a pension in a month.'

'It's the only way you can make money in police work,' I said. 'Put in twenty years with one department, draw a half-pay pension, and then get a full-time job in another department. The way it is over there, a new town opens up every day, it seems like. They all need policing. Nil give you my address?'

'Well, I can get it from him.'

Over Withers's shoulder, I could see the car, Ralph moving restlessly, Miss Beaumont talking, slowly and softly. The rubber band that held us alive was stretching too damned thin; but I couldn't hurry this. I took out my Naranjo Vista I.D. and let him copy what he wanted. Writing, he asked: 'Three-platoon system over there?'

'Three and a relief platoon. Forty-two hours duty a week, overtime at pay and a half.'

'Sounds like a piece of cake . . . Nil said you held a badge with the Feds, too.'

'Army C.I.D.,' I said. 'I do a job once in a while on my time off.'

'Oh?' He looked at me. Slowly I took my army I.D. out, too. He took it from me, read the front, read the back. I'd been right; this was no casual stop. He had said that three-platoon work was a piece of cake, and I have never heard an

American say that unless he has had duty with the British army. No Arizona state assignment would give him that contact, so he was army himself — or maybe air force; and had been told to stop us so he could see if the army card — which he probably carried himself — was real. He copied nothing off it in front of me, but as he handed it back he said: 'Major's pretty good.'

'You an old army man yourself?' The load was lifting. My I.D. card was authentic as J. Edgar Hoover's.

He just shrugged and held out his hand. We exchanged the usual parting messages, and he turned around, gave a hard stare at the windshield of the Cad, and then walked ahead to his cruiser.

I got behind the wheel again. Ralph was babbling. 'I don't like the way he looked at me! They have no right, honest, they're all just bullies and big shots, after all.'

The Cadillac was moving. I pulled out and around Withers, waving my hand out the window. It was impossible to tell how much he'd seen. I cut a sharp voice at

Ralph, desperately trying to pipe him down; Withers would be following us, and Ralph was jerking around with a wildness that would look weird through the back window.

'Me, Ralph? I'm a police officer — am I a bully and a big shot?'

'Yeah,' he screeched. 'You're a lousy, lying detective. I know how it is, I've read about it. Act friendly with a fellow, and get him to talk, tell his old buddy the detective everything he knows. I know just how it is.'

Miss Beaumont had squinched up between us again, trying to disappear.

I had to keep this going. We had tried many methods of calming Ralph; maybe the hardman act would do it. Meanwhile, we were eating the last few miles of Arizona; Jake Withers, riding my rear-view mirror, would have to turn back. 'You know how it is,' I snapped. 'You know everything, from reading books! It's time to live a little, Ralph, and find out something for yourself; time to get your nose out of the books and see things.'

He settled down and grabbed the edge

of the seat on either side of his thighs, hanging on tight. 'All right! I'll see the world. Just let me out of this car and I'll see the world. I'd jump if there was just a handle here, but you stole the handle, Lieutenant Bastian. That's what — '

A sign on the highway shoulder. 'Welcome to New Mexico.' Real pretty sign, yellow and red; I'd never known before they were my favorite colors. The pavement got rougher under our wheels, and we were in New Mexico.

The rear-view mirror showed Patrolman Jake Withers waving and turning back. I looked, but there was no New Mexico patrol car ready to pick us up; and again, maybe, I'd pulled my hand back from lukewarm water to avoid being scalded.

Starting to relax, I viewed the scenery. It seems ridiculous, but New Mexico looked different from Arizona. There were beautiful soft red cliffs looming off to the left; and it had rained here, and there was green covering the red soil thinly. Out on the flat, between the cliffs and 66, a turquoise blue truck was crawling towards the highway, following a pair of blood-red ruts. Everything was just gorgeous.

I said: 'Ralph, I'm sorry. You were going into hysterics; I thought a little hard lip might snap you out of it.'

His eyes were dull as he slumped in his seat. 'It doesn't matter.'

Miss Beaumont seemed to be expanding again. I felt her thigh soft against mine. I said: 'Miss Beaumont, Ralph's trying to beat my time. He bought you a souvenir of Arizona, it's my turn to buy you one of New Mexico. If he'll help me; I don't know beans about turquoise. I don't even know if that's what you ought to buy in New Mexico.'

Ralph didn't rise to the bait. Miss Beaumont gamely took her licks. 'The women back at college won't believe me,' she said, 'when I come back jingling with jewelry. They'll think I've been holding up filling stations along the way.'

Unexpectedly, that reached the boy. 'Hey, how would you go about holding up a filling station, Andy? I'll bet all the years you've been a policeman, you've seen about every way there is. I'll bet you could manage a stickup and get away with it slick as axle grease.'

There wasn't enough energy in me to dream up a straight answer to that. I wasn't up to giving a lecture on modus operandi just then. Instead, I started a long and dull story about three GIs who robbed a bunch of pubs in England in 1943. It had been my first assignment to criminal investigations, and like the first anything, I remembered every detail. There were enough of them and they were boring enough to put him sound asleep before we passed the Gallup city limits.

Miss Beaumont said softly: 'We'd better eat and then walk around Gallup a little.'

'Well, we're making better progress than an oxcart, anyway.'

'Andy, oxcarts went west, not east.'

Ralph woke up with a start. 'How about the Santa Fe Trail, huh? Oxcarts went both ways on it, didn't they? Of course, it runs from northeast to southwest. But I'll betcha oxcarts freighted stuff from California to Arizona. Maybe they used mules mostly, but I'll bet there were some oxcarts.'

Suddenly I was laughing. 'Ralph, there's no one like you in the world.'

Miss Beaumont was laughing, too. 'Back when they had quiz shows that weren't rigged, Ralph would have made our fortune.'

'How about that?' he asked. 'Hey, let's each say what he'd do if he had a million dollars. How about you, Andy?'

We were in the middle of Gallup now. On the left there was a railroad track backed by big warehouses; on the right, block after block of mean little shops. The sidewalk was crowded; people were crossing the tracks to the warehouse district. There were maybe ten Indians to every white person. The men were dressed in bright cowboy shirts, black hats and bluejeans; the women in full skirts and velveteen blouses. Both sexes and all ages were covered with silver and turquoise jewelry.

Occasionally one of the Indians would be bareheaded, long hair tied up with a bright strand of wool. They might have been old-style Indians, or they might have been from a different tribe or nation; I was no expert. Of course, I could have asked Ralph and gotten a full course on the ethnology and history of the American Indian, from the north pole to Patagonia, but just then Gallup opened up a little, and I saw a couple of restaurants. I chose one that looked fairly clean and had big plate-glass windows, and brought the Cadillac to a halt.

There was no longer any need for conversation between Miss Beaumont and me. She headed for a front table where we could watch the car without my saying a word and waited at there, watching, till Ralph and I got back from the men's room; and only then did she go to powder her nose.

A bleached-blonde 66-type waitress brought us menus. Ralph looked at his and went, as he would have said, winging away. 'Hey, this place is half-Chinese and half-Italian,' he said after one of his quick careless looks. 'Six different kinds of spaghetti and four kinds of chow mein.'

Limping along behind him, I said: 'Enchiladas and something called chile rellenos, too, if you'll pardon my accent. What do you make of that?'

Ralph dismissed my little contribution without thought. 'Oh, every place in New Mexico serves those,' he said. 'Chile rellenos are green chiles stuffed with cheese and fried in egg . . . I had them coming across here once when I was a kid. Chinese and Italian food, now, that's significant. Hey, Andy, let's make a bet. I'll bet this restaurant's owned by a Chinese man with an Italian wife.'

'Okay,' I said. 'I'll bet the other way around. Italian man with a Chinese wife.'

Miss Beaumont went along with keeping Ralph happy. 'I'll bet it's a Chinese who used to work for an Italian restaurant.'

Ralph said: 'Hey, I never thought of that . . . What are we betting?'

'The two losers have to call the winner worshipful master till suppertime.' That was Miss Beaumont, recalling something from her childhood, no doubt.

'Hey,' Ralph said, 'I hope I win.'

He bounced a little in his chair as the waitress approached, bringing us the answer to the mystery. But I was out of

213

the game. A man had come around the corner of the restaurant building, and had walked up to the Cadillac; he looked at the license plate, and then at the registration slip on the steering wheel. Here we went again.

The waitress was at our table; Ralph was saying: 'Hey, who owns this restaurant? Is he — '

I muttered some sort of apology and slipped out from behind my seat. The restaurant was air-conditioned; the minute I stepped outside, the hard heat was banging on my head. I walked over to the car.

'Looking for something, friend?' It was my full cop's voice.

He straightened up and gave me a stare. He was no cream-puff: a man about six feet tall, spare and broad-shouldered, with very small eyes in which I could read nothing at all. He said: 'I'm looking for a Lieutenant Bastian, or a Major Bastian, depending on how you read it; but it says here this is a Mr. Bartlett's rig.'

'I'm driving it,' I said. 'I'll answer for it.'

'Bastian?' He hardly waited for my nod

before he had a badge out of his pocket and was flashing it. 'We'd like to talk to you downtown.'

'Downtown. In Gallup?'

This was no word-waster. 'Yep.'

'You mean a town this size has that kind of police force?'

His hand was half-under his coat in front. Belt holster; and he looked like he knew how to use it. 'We're proud of Gallup, mister. And if you don't think that a town where twenty thousand Indians do their drinking doesn't need a big police department, you're wrong.'

'All right.' I smiled, and got no change back from him. 'I'm about to order my lunch. When I've finished eating it, I'll drop down and see you.'

His look was pure amazement. 'Mister, when the chief says come see him, you don't eat first.'

When I reached for my left hip, he didn't draw; he didn't have to. His long-barreled .38 was in a swivel holster with no bottom to it; he could shoot without drawing. I shook my head at him and got my wallet out. 'I carry all kinds of

I.D.,' I said. 'If your chief wants to see me, that's fine. But a little professional courtesy never hurt any man's department.'

He kept the gun on me. 'I just work here,' he said. 'The chief tells me what to do. If you can prove you're Bastian, that's fine. But we got word that Lieutenant Bastian is dead, found in a field back in California, and that you're traveling with his papers.'

'My fingerprints are — '

'Downtown. I couldn't take fingerprints out here on 66, could I? Listen, mister, if you're clean, you could be back here in the time you're spending arguing with me.'

So I shrugged, turned and waved a hand at Miss Beaumont; Ralph was talking with a full mouth and didn't notice me. Then I said: 'Your car or mine?'

'Why use your gas? The city car's around back.' He gestured with the hand that didn't stay near his belt gun. I walked along the front of the restaurant, traffic whizzing and snorting and whirring on my right side. I said: 'I should think you'd get tired of the smell of 66 running through your town.'

He was very good. He said: 'We make our living off it.'

'And the Indians?'

'Sure. And the Indians.'

'I thought there were special Indian police.' I turned the corner and went along the blank sidewall of the restaurant, up an alley. There was another blank wall on the other side; I remembered that it belonged to a garage. The heat was worse in the alley, cut off from the breeze.

Ahead was the back area of the restaurant; I could hear clanging and banging and I could smell garbagey smells.

Then I couldn't hear or see anything, couldn't smell anything; all of Gallup went away, and for a second or less I could feel a terrible sharp pain in my head. And then I couldn't feel anything at all.

15

Considering the life I've led, it is funny that I had never been socked over the head before. It is an experience I cannot recommend to anyone. I came to, if that's where I came, in little pieces. I was covered with cold sweat, and shaking all over.

My fingers explored my hair and were surprised to remain dry. Somehow or other I remembered being socked with a gun barrel, which made no sense at all because I was hit from behind, never saw it coming and —

After a while I could stand up. At once I wished I hadn't, and leaned against the alley wall. My stomach kept trying to empty itself, and couldn't because I'd been knocked over before I'd had my lunch.

When I could navigate with reasonable precision, I went out to the front of the restaurant. There were a half dozen cars parked there, and one of them was the Cadillac. Nothing had ever surprised me so much in my life.

I turned slowly, because my turning mechanism had been damaged. Miss Beaumont and Ralph were not behind the plate-glass window. I hadn't thought they would be.

So now I knew what this was all about. A simple snatch. The cheesewits in the maroon Buick had been trailing us because Ralph's father was rich. A ransom job.

Just the sort of thing a cheesewit would try. They didn't have a prayer. Kidnapping is as serious as murder in the eyes of any cop in the country. All I had to do was get downtown to the Gallup police station and use their wires, and every road in this open endless country would be closed in a few minutes.

My map unrolled in my head. West was the road we'd come in on, old 66, forty-one miles to the junction that went down to Apache country, Springerville and Show Low and so on. I remembered it well, because I'd sweated it out towards that junction when I thought the cheesewits had damaged the Cad.

East 66 went to Grants. There were turnoffs, but they were just dirt roads. North went 666, and there were ninety-three miles of it before Shiprock, the first paved turnoff. South, I wasn't too sure. There was a road that went to the Zuñi reservation, but if it dead-ended there, I couldn't remember. It's name was 32 though, that I knew: State Highway 32. The things a policeman can remember!

As though he'd read my battered brain, a man beside me said: 'You're a trained officer, Lieutenant Bastian. Which way did they go?'

Dropping dead from surprise is not my style, so I didn't. I hadn't known he or anyone was there; and I certainly hadn't expected anyone to read my mind. At first I didn't know him. Just a small Indian in a light blue work shirt, dark blue jeans, a flat gray cowboy hat. Then I made him. I said: 'What are you doing here, Mr. Cuero?'

He shrugged. 'I don' think those boys over in Cupra are gonna catch the fella who beat my girl,' he said. There was no change of expression on his face when he mentioned his daughter, none at all. 'They tol' me to go away, go back to keepin' law'n order on the reservation. So I took off. I'm not satisfied with what you told Patrolman Nilsen about your boy. He looks like a bad boy to me, maybe crazy. I'm sorry for a poor crazy boy, but he shouldn't hurt my girl.'

This was real crazy, this standing in the hot sun with my aching head, listening to this Indian. I said: 'He didn't hit your girl. Or anybody.' I had to come a little cleaner. 'He's a sick boy, yes. Maybe you'd call him crazy. But he thought he'd hit the girl in the mouth, and there wasn't a mark on his hands. You can believe me or not, but he didn't do it.'

Bob Cuero nodded. 'Yeah, I know that now. What happened here?'

My voice was slow coming out. I was very tired. 'I don't know.'

He cracked at me in his guttural tones. 'You been hit on the head, okay. But now you pull together, Lieutenant. You're a real law officer. I'm just a fellow who picks up drunks on the reservation.' It was the one word he said clearly; the rest were slurred with what I guess is an Indian accent; I had never talked to enough Indians to know. 'You're a real law officer. Look over these cars, look at the road; you can tell if any cars pulled out of here in the last few minutes.'

'But I don't even know how long I was out. A man showed me a badge, I walked up the alley, and he knocked me out.'

'When I don't know what time it is,' Bob Cuero said, 'I look at my watch.'

I looked at mine. 'It's only been five minutes!'

'Sure. Now look for tire marks. You got the trainin'.'

That was right. I'd all the training that was needed. Most officers can't tell how old tire marks are except policemen who have just gotten out of traffic investigation school, but I have this memory; it had carried me from private to major in the military police, and gotten me my good job at Naranjo Vista.

So I got down on my haunches and examined the parking in front of the restaurant. Doing that sent blood up to my head, and for a minute my vision was red; then I could see.

It wasn't a very difficult job. There were a number of marks where tires had put their prints, going east, going west. There was a steady flow of dust building up in the prints. With lab equipment I could have measured it; but I really didn't need to, since I wasn't going to have to testify in a court of law. The prints filled with dust at a rate that was easily discernible; you could see it happening. A five-minute-old print was a third full; a fifteen-minute one would look old.

There was no necessity to point this out to Bob Cuero; for some reason I didn't know, he had faith in my professional ability, if not in my truthfulness. I stood up. 'Only one car out of here in the last half hour.' It had gone east, away from Gallup.

I pointed it out to Bob Cuero, and he nodded and said: 'C'mon.'

I got behind the wheel of the Cadillac, and when he was in next to me, I started up. But I headed into Gallup.

Bob Cuero said: 'Them tracks went the other way.'

'They were following me in a car that had regular tires. The tracks showed they have snow tires now. What some call mud tires.'

'Reservation tires, we call 'em,' Bob Cuero said.

We both meant the same thing; rubber with big cleats on it to take hold in loose traction.

Bob Cuero said: 'Not so many car dealers in Gallup we can't find out what they're wheelin' now . . . How come you give Nilsen a snow job?'

'The boy's father paid me to deliver him to a hospital in Kansas. If he was questioned by cops, it might make him come completely apart. He's pretty nervous.'

'How come you don't give me a snow job?'

'You wouldn't fall for it.'

'Yeah,' he said. 'I'm checkin' it back to you, Lieutenant. You got the trainin'. I'm ridin' along, is all. When we get them, I want the one with the tooth marks on his hands. She didn't have no teeth left in her mouth, they was all knocked loose.'

'Nilsen should have thought of that,' I said.

'Well, your boy could have worn gloves. On'y I don' think so, now. I think they was gonna take your boy in Cupra, and my girl, she got in the way, is what I think.' It was almost t'ink, but not quite. 'What we gone do, Lieutenant, when we find what car they're runnin'?'

That was a good question. I let it lie between us a few seconds, and tried one on for size. 'I still don't want my boy questioned. I think you want to make a one-man pinch. So if we don't yell copper?'

He waited more time than I had to answer. Then he said: 'Jake with me, Lieutenant.'

The second dealer we talked to had sold the cheesewits a four-door two-year-old gray Chevrolet. He'd taken the Buick and five hundred dollars in trade, and felt pretty pleased with himself. We left him wondering whether the money or the Buick had been stolen. I was mean enough to let him worry; he was that kind of a used-car dealer.

We headed east again. I wondered if I'd lied to him about doing this myself to protect Ralph. Maybe my real reason was not so noble; maybe it was purely selfish. If we got on the air with a great big splash, Mr. Bartlett would not get the privacy he had bought from me, and I would be out of my soft job at Naranjo Vista.

I tried hard not to think of Miss Beaumont and Ralph. Maybe they wouldn't hurt the boy, but they had no reason not to heave Miss Beaumont out on her ear as soon as they were out of sight of the heavy traffic of 66.

I said: 'Bob, give the map a quick reading. They'd get off the highways as soon as possible, even if they are cheese-wits.' I gave him the key to the glove compartment.

'Cheesewits? What's that?'

'A halfwit has half a brain in his head. A cheesewit has nothing but inexpensive, slightly spoiled cottage cheese.'

He laughed. 'Sounds like a word in my

language. We got lots of words end that way. Inyatz, now, that means both me an' the sun.' He rattled the map, studying it. 'Lots of little roads, mebbe more than are on this map, but they'd want one that goes someplace.'

'Yeah. They might even know the country. Lots of cheesewits are Indian lovers. The dame was wearing what looked like Navajo jewelry.'

He grunted. 'Slow down, Lieutenant. Road coming up on the left.' He snapped the map shut. 'There, right by that sign.' The sign said 'Kit Carson's Cave,' and some stuff under it for tourists. The side road was paved for a bare fifty feet, just enough to protect 66 from having too much mud tracked onto it. I stopped where the apron ended and the dirt road began. It looked pretty rough ahead.

Bob Cuero hopped out of the car and knelt on the edge of the apron. 'Car with reservation tires went through here,' he said. 'Can't tell how long ago.'

'We'll take a chance,' I said. 'They wouldn't stay on the highways very long. Four patrolmen could block them in.'

He hopped back in the car, and then suddenly laughed as I started up again. 'This Cadillac's gonna take a beatin',' he said. 'Reservation roads, they run plenty rough. If they're on this road, we'll get them. Only three roads around here go anyplace. If we don't break down.'

Snapping the lever into a lower cluster of gears, I nodded. 'With these springs, this motor, we can cut down their lead. You got a gun, Bob?'

'Little gun, short-nose .38. They take yours when they knock you out?'

'Sure.'

He nodded, staring out at the stunted trees, the red rocks of the scenery. 'What I figger. Get rid of you, and the woman an' boy are a cinch to take. Mebbe we shoulda told the cops; gotten the FBI.'

All I could answer to that was a shrug. My spirits were rising again, though my head still had a bad ache. We were going to get them. They weren't very smart, and they weren't very tough; just hard-talking, two of them. The one I'd pulled out of the pool wasn't even that, and the woman didn't amount to anything at all.

The rear-view mirror showed me nothing but a cloud of red dust. It hung on both sides of the car, but too far back to obscure our side view; ahead it was clear as a vodka bottle. I said: 'They'd put up a cloud of dust like ours.'

Bob Cuero shrugged. 'I thought of that. But there's trucks movin' aroun' the reservation, an' mebby-so guys ploughing, and then there's dust-devils, look jus' like a car when you're twenty miles away.'

The dust around us turned from red to pure white, and we bucketed up a hill. The Cad was acting like it had never been on a highway in its life, like this was its natural habitat. But the paint job was taking a terrible beating from the pebbles we were knocking around.

Then another dust cloud came towards us, and Bob Cuero said: 'Better stop.'

As soon as I did, he hopped out, pinning on his Indian service badge and giving it a quick unconscious polish with the flat of his hand.

A red pickup came towards us, trailing red dust and then white dust as it hit the patch of caliche we were in. The men in the pickup saw Bob and skidded to a halt; that road was as slick as talcum powder.

Bob Cuero leaned on the side of the cab and talked to the men. They answered; then all three of them, the two Navajos in the truck and Cuero, started waving their hands. Then he shrugged angrily and walked back, and they drove past us, showering us with dust.

He got back in. 'G'wan. They didn't talk enough English for me to learn nothin'.'

'Don't you speak their language?'

He said: 'Hell, *no*. I don't speak no Indian but my own language, and not much of that, no more.' He seemed mad about something 'They knew what Chevrolet was, an' they said somethin' about one, but I dunno.'

'What are you mad about?'

'They called me a lousy fish-eater. Navajos think they're better than anybody in the worl'.'

We came out of the caliche and into a land of pink: pink rocks, pink soil, pink gravel on the road and pink-edged clouds building up in the distant sky. Even the trees, junipers I guess, had pink bark, and very green leaves. It was beautiful in a sort of frightening way.

Bob Cuero looked at the clouds and said: 'Mebbe we oughta have reservation tires. If this was my country, I'd say it was gonna rain, but I don't know this Navajo land. Mebbe the same signs don't mean nothin' here.'

The road twisted, the soil went from pink to red, and then there was an irrigated field, the first I'd seen. Bob Cuero looked at the thick green plants. 'Milo maize.' He shrugged. 'Indians don't like to farm, mostly. They tell me the people in the pueblos, Hopi an' over east, they like to plough, but I dunno.'

Cattle had pushed up against the barbed-wire fence around the milo maize, trying to get off the rocky desert land to the lush irrigated growth. I drifted the Cadillac down to twenty and then ten miles an hour, avoiding the cattle; some of the cows had calves at their sides.

'Navajo gettin' plenty rich,' Bob Cuero said. 'Oil an' gas an' uranium.' He seemed unhappy and mad, and I had expected he'd sort of blossom out on a reservation, where he had more right than a white man. But it was the other way around.

Past the little green patch, the cattle thinned out and then left the road altogether. We went through another juniper grove and came out where bunch grass grew with reasonable frequency. A bunch of sheep were off to one side, and a dog left them to come barking and chasing our car; a little Navajo woman on a horse hid her face as we went by.

Then we went over some hills and past a couple of dried-up reservoirs, the mud caking and cracking in their fenced-in areas. Abruptly we went around a curve, and there was a black panel truck there, like the one I'd seen Bob Cuero drive in Cupra. It said 'Police' and had a red spotlight, and was parked twenty feet from a trading post.

When I stepped on the brake, the Cad skidded just as the pickup had done. This dust was as slick as wet blacktop. I pulled up alongside the Indian police truck, and said: 'Maybe you better talk to them, Bob.'

'Hope they speak a little English,' he said, apparently still mad because the Navajo boys had snubbed him.

His hope was granted; one of the two men in the truck was white, at least to my eye. He was wearing a green uniform with gold bars on his shoulders. The other officer was an Indian with no mark of rank, just his Navajo police badge.

Bob gave the captain a salute that he had not learned on any reservation. 'We're lookin' for some people, Captain. Driving a four-door Chevy, year before last's; reservation tires on th' rear.'

The captain was a cowboy-looking type. He grunted. The Navajo patrolman said: 'You got no right to wear that badge on Navajo land, mister.'

Bob Cuero gulped and said: 'This isn't a pinch.' He reached up and took his badge off. 'Anyway, way I heard it, a Navajo's gotta get the FBI to pinch a non-Indian on th' reservation. We jus' got a message for them, my old army buddy and me here.'

'They went by here about fifteen minutes ago,' the captain said. He talked as though every word cost him a day's pay. 'Heading for Cedar Ridge.'

'Check,' Bob Cuero said, 'an' thanks, Captain.'

The captain nodded gravely. We went back to the Cadillac and took off again. Bob Cuero said: 'He coulda offered to radio ahead. But Navajos, they won't give you the time o' day. And the white Navajos, they're the worst of all.'

'Was that captain a white Navajo?'

'Sure, white man who works for the tribe.'

A puff of cool air came across the land and into the car; then the sun went behind a cloud, and we were cold. In this dry land, there was nothing. Bob Cuero had been struggling with the map; he folded it and put it away.

'Looks like there's no fork between here an' Cedar Ridge, but then none of these maps got all the Indian roads on 'em. Lieutenant, it's gonna rain.'

'If it rains on us, it rains on them.'

He grunted. 'You don' know this country like I do. It can pick out one side of a house to rain on, leave the sun peelin'' the paint off the other side.'

We went over a high ridge covered with junipers and stunted pine trees and down the other side in a cloud of dust that got tricky and went ahead of us, choking us. We cranked up our windows in a hurry.

'This is high country,' I said.

'Snow country,' Bob Cuero agreed. He pointed a finger at the red snow fence above the road. 'Not this time of year, though.' He shook his head. 'Jus' rain.' He laughed. 'Hope the Hopis over west haven't been doin' a dance. They do strong rain dances.'

'What kind of people are they?'

'Aw, Hopis get along with everybody.' He twisted in his seat. 'What's wrong with that boy you had wit' you?'

'Nervous,' I said. 'Just very nervous.' Which would have described me just then. Since the trading post and the Indian police car, we had passed nobody at all; we had seen nothing move except very, very distant cattle — maybe they were horses, I couldn't tell at that distance — out on the edge of the mesas.

This quiet, rather bitter man next to

me had a gun, and I didn't. And it seemed to me that he'd been too damned agreeable; and maybe I had, too. Never having been knocked over the head before, I didn't know if it made a man stupid for a while, but it seemed reasonable; a blow hard enough to make my neck still shouldn't be calculated to make my brain work better.

I'd gone along with him, I'd let him turn me off 66 into this howling wasteland, and to what end? If he thought Ralph had hurt his daughter, he might want to take revenge on me. Maybe he thought I had beaten the girl. I sure couldn't read anything in his face.

Even the stunted cedars and piñons were gone, and we bucketed down a hill on a straight road lined only with rocks that no longer shone, now that the clouds had covered the sun. Then at the bottom, the road suddenly turned right, and I almost skidded the Cadillac into a ditch making the twist.

I was still fighting the wheel when a fork opened up ahead of us, the first since the highway. 'Take the left hand,' Bob

Cuero said, and I rammed all my weight into the wheel and cut to the right; despite the remains of a bad headache, I was myself again, and determined to dominate the situation.

All of which got me about a hundred yards before I had to put all my weight on the brake to keep from hitting a cyclone fence's locked gate.

'Wrong turn, Lieutenant,' Bob Cuero said. I'd stalled the motor, but I made no move to start it up again; I tried to relax in my seat and stare at the dark man as he said: 'This just goes to a reservoir. You gotta have a key.'

Now was the time to get control. I said: 'Bob, where are we going?'

'After the people in the gray Chevrolet.'

'Why?'

He stared through the multi-colored dust on the windshield. 'You want to get your boy back. Me, I want to see if any of the fellows in the Chevy, they got marks on them from beating my woman.'

'And where'll we find them?'

He shrugged. 'I been looking at the map. There's two roads go outa Cedar

Ridge, one up north through Chaco Canyon and out to a highway; one back down to 66 at a place called Thoreau.' He pronounced it exactly Through, and all the time I was off the highways, I never heard it pronounced any other way. 'Mebbe there's other roads. Mebbe they got friends at Cedar Ridge. We better get outa here — here comes the rain.'

He pointed with a steady finger, and I saw the hard slanting lines coming towards us. I started the motor, backed up, and went back to the fork, and this time I took the turn he'd told me to in the first place. We'd lost about ten minutes.

16

Driving hard on the road from the little reservoir to Cedar Ridge, the rain followed us, and after ten minutes it caught up with us; a gentle rain, shoved into sloping by the wind, but not coming down very hard.

Five minutes of that, and the car was fighting me. Like every other American, I take great pride in my driving; a little mud couldn't daunt me. I did all the right things, keeping my feet off the brakes, shifting the automatic drive into low, turning the wheels towards the skids instead of away from them, and so we kept going — at a dandy, elaborate five miles an hour. The speedometer, of course, said more, because our wheels were going around fast in the slick. Twice pickups passed us and spattered us with red mud or gray mud, plentifully mixed with pebbles. Mr. Bartlett's Cadillac would never be the same.

Bob Cuero rattled the map, and it annoyed me. But I couldn't take my eyes off the road long enough to frown at him; every so often the left or right side would look more solid than the other, and I'd try and get there to take advantage of rock or sand, or anything but the excellent Navajo brand of clay.

He said: 'Now pretty soon we go through a pass, an' mebbe the pass'll be rocky; lots of 'em are. Satan's Pass, they call it on the map.'

'Sounds hospitable.'

'Yeah.'

Real trees clustered around the western entrance to Satan's Pass, pines and maybe firs; I didn't stop to collect needles and bark. The Cad held the road a little better, and then we went over the ridge and started down.

By then I was swearing in all the languages of all the countries I'd ever been stationed in: German, Korean, French, Japanese, Dutch and a few others. Some of the languages didn't have many swear words, others were rich in them. I used English to fill in the chinks.

Satan's Pass road had had its back broken by some anti-Navajo like Bob Cuero. It had died in agony, and I died all over again coming down it. There wasn't a stretch of a hundred feet that went straight; first right, then left, but always down. We lost altitude so fast that my ears would have popped if it hadn't been for my nervous swallowing every couple of seconds.

We went through a couple of gaudy-colored puddles that mired up the windshield, but Mr. Bartlett and Mr. Cadillac had provided the car with one of those water squirters, and I didn't have to drive blind very long. There were no Navajos on the road; they had better sense.

Then, thank God, we were out of Satan's Pass and making one final twist, and there was a straightaway ahead of us. I said: 'Bob, did my hair turn white?'

He said: 'I dunno what language you was prayin' in, but tell me and I'll join your church.'

'That wasn't praying, it was swearing.'

'I'll join the Swear Church, then. We

ain't more than five miles out of Cedar Ridge.'

'Bob, you really think they're ahead of us?'

He nodded. 'Yeah. I t'ought so when we saw the tire marks turning off . . . Lieutenant, you're a kind of a frightening guy. They wouldn't stay on the highway with you following them.'

'But there could have been other turnoffs.'

He regarded the windshield wipers for a while. Then he said: 'Gov'ment don't put no more roads on reservations than it's got to. I know, and you don' know, and mebbe I wish I'd never learned. It's no kind of life, on most reservations.'

I was still driving slow, still fighting the slick clay, so I couldn't look at him. 'Why do you stick it, Bob?'

'They're my people,' he said.

The rain, having had its licks at us in Satan's Pass, went away, and we could see. Off across the mesa was a clump of green and a white splotch under it; trees and a house. A few of the slab-sided hogans of the Navajos dotted the country, too; we were no longer completely alone. But the road was still wet and slippery, and I drove with caution; maybe we were making ten miles an hour then.

Finally, there were the houses of Cedar Ridge, and we had made it. Of course, there was no reason to suppose the cheesewits had come to Cedar Ridge, or, if they had, were still there. All I knew was that I was following a couple of snow tires, or Bob Cuero said I was. It didn't seem any way for a practiced police officer to be conducting himself, for all Bob's reassurances.

One final skid, and then we were in the metropolis of Cedar Ridge: a trading post, a horrible-looking little restaurant, a jail around which clustered three of the Indian service black marias or cruisers or whatever they called them. I flipped at them with my thumb. 'More of your friends, Bob.'

He said: 'I talked to all the Navajos I need to. We'll drive around this place; if th' Chevy's here, we'll see it.'

'And if it isn't?'

'Then we take off again. We gonna find

those people, them cheesewits you told me about. Cheesewits,' he said, turning the word over for flavor.

So we drove around Cedar Ridge, the great tour. Another trading post, a Dutch Reform mission, a community house apparently locked up, with Navajos lounging on the outside. A government agency with a lawn and nice trees and water spraying; it hadn't rained here. We saw a lot of cars, mostly pickups and other light trucks, some station wagons, a few sedans. Some of them were Chevrolets, but the gray ones were the wrong year, or were two doors instead of four.

'Something down there,' I said. It was dusk, and lights were going on. I drove the battered Cadillac towards them.

It was a school, a big good-looking school, and behind it what looked like a suburban apartment house, one of the sprawled-out kind they have in California and the southwest, very snappy, very modern, as decorative as a crushed fingernail in this godforsaken desert. There were lights in several of the windows and there were cars parked around. There was a pool of water that had run off from the watered lawn.

The Cadillac splashed through the pool of water, and there was a gray four-door two-year-old Chevrolet. I brought the Cadillac to a quivering halt, and we got out.

As we walked away from Mr. Bartlett's six thousand dollars' worth of coupé, I looked back at it. Sometime, someplace — probably coming down Satan's Pass — I'd grazed the right rear fender on something, a rock or a tree. A new fender was indicated. Well, the right-hand door could have stood a cleaning and pressing. It rippled like water in a spring breeze.

Bob Cuero saw where I was looking, and grinned. 'That was up on the mesa, before we went into the pass. A piñon. I thought it was comin' into my lap.'

'Next time I come up this way, I'll hire a chauffeur.'

'Reservation tires is more to the point. That Chevy's got them.'

His steady hand pointed. I nodded. 'They got through before the rain, from the looks. But we caught up with them.'

'Sure, they gotta be in one of the rooms here.' The word 'apartment' was probably unknown to him. 'Now we use you. A real city police man.'

But I didn't feel real, citified, or like a policeman. We'd caught up with the cheesewits, and all I felt was scared of what we'd find next. There'd been a thousand opportunities to dump a body on the road we'd come over. A body that had been named Miss Beaumont, a body that had been named Ralph.

A young woman answered the first door I knocked on. Behind her, a young man sat in an overstuffed chair, reading a book; a little boy was pushing a fire truck around on the plastic tile floor. I asked her if she knew which apartment owned the gray Chevrolet.

She said: 'No, I'm sorry. I never saw it before.' She turned. 'Paul, do you know anything about a gray Chevrolet outside?'

Paul raised his head from the book. 'No. But if it's in good shape, it doesn't belong here.'

His wife laughed. 'Sorry. Would the people you're looking for be Indians? The

246

teachers in the next apartment are Navajo.'

Bob grunted.

I said: 'Well, we'll try around, and thank you.'

Out in what was now full dark, we peered at each other. I said: 'If we swing and miss too often, they'll hear us.'

'Let's skip the Indian teachers.'

'The cheesewit woman had a lot of Indian jewelry on. She could have Navajo friends.'

Bob Cuero said: 'We can always come back.' He had as bad a case of racial prejudice as I had ever encountered, if you can call the feeling between two kinds of Indians that.

So I knocked two doors down. The next three apartments were dark. After a moment, the door opened, and a small, trim woman came out and stood looking up at me. This was no cheesewit. Her eyes were clear and the lines of her face showed character; her jutting chin was firm under her thin lips. Her slightly graying hair was pulled back in a serviceable bun.

I said: 'Police officers, ma'am,' like that fellow who used to be on the radio. She was not one to fool around with. 'We're looking for the people who parked a gray sedan, Chevrolet, just outside here.'

She looked at me, she looked at Bob Cuero. She dropped her eyes to his badge. 'You're a special officer from the Hualpai Reservation,' she said, reading the badge. 'What are you doing here?'

As clearly as though he'd spoken, I could hear his thought: *White Navajos is the worst of all.* I managed not to smile, and said: 'Just about the Chevrolet, ma'am, and we won't bother you further.'

She said: 'There's no need to call me ma'am. My name is Miss Fell. Dr. Fell, though I don't use the title. I'm in charge of visual aids at the school here. And unless I see something more legal than a Hualpai badge in a Navajo town, I have no intention of answering any questions at all.'

This was no dame to fall for an army reserve card; and my Naranjo Vista shield would send her screaming for the Navajo black marias. I said: 'A question about a car is not the third degree, Miss Fell.'

'Then you have no legal status in Navajo country.' It was not a question.

Bob Cuero said: 'You better answer the lieutenant's questions, lady.'

She asked: 'Why?' and then shut her mouth. This was no cheesewit, but it was getting to be kind of certain that she was in some way connected with them. Bob Cuero got it, and I could feel him move beside me, and then suddenly his stocky body was moving forward, and against the thin woman's. She either had to step aside or be walked on. She stepped aside. I followed Bob Cuero in, and she followed me.

We were in a living room identical with the one the married teachers had been in, except for furniture. This dame was one of the moderns; steamed wood and ceramic tile and so on.

There was no one there except us chickens.

Bob Cuero was mad. It didn't show in his face — nothing ever showed there — but in the slam of his heels between the islands that Navajo rugs made on the

249

tiled floor. He went slamming around a corner of the living room, then slammed back, putting his hand on a telephone table to steady his turn. 'Nothing there. Kitchen.' He threw open a door. I could see into a bathroom, but that didn't satisfy Bob Cuero; he marched in there and flipped the shower curtain back.

Another door. I watched him go through it; so did the woman, Miss Fell. There were white spots alongside her nose now, anger spots. One of her sensible shoes moved restlessly, as though she wanted to tap her foot. I had never seen anyone but an actress indicate impatience that way.

Bob Cuero came back. 'Nothin'.'

Miss Fell said: 'Did you look in my closets? How about my bureau drawers? Did you look under the bed?'

Bob Cuero said: 'The bedspring's flat on the floor . . . Nothin' here, lieutenant. I guess she's just a cop hater.'

I said: 'Bob, get out and watch the Chevrolet. Watch all the cars out there.' I tossed the keys to the Cadillac in my hand. 'We don't want them getting away.' When he was gone, I said: 'Now, Miss

Fell. Where are they?'

'Who?' She walked across the room to the telephone table. 'The jail's right up by the community house. The Navajo officers can be here in a minute.'

'If you'd been going to call them, you'd have done it when Bob Cuero started searching your room. You don't look to me like a lady who can be pushed around. So — you don't want the police in on this any more than I do.'

'Then you admit you're not a policeman? That this is illegal entry?'

Except for the Navajo rugs on the floor, there was nothing in that living room to absorb sound. My voice bounced back from the walls and ceiling as I cut it at her. 'Stop this horsing around! I'm a cop all right, a damned tough cop. I'm looking for people who've beaten a girl and kidnapped a boy — I'm looking for a sick kid they're holding and a woman worth ten of you!'

Her eyes had gotten wide, maybe for the first time in her mature life. She backed away from the telephone table and against the wall, just before the turn into the kitchenette. Finally, she whispered: 'They're down the row.'

'Down the row?'

'Second apartment down. It's empty. It belongs to a doctor who's covering Fort Defiance for a week, a friend of mine.' She raised her thin face. 'You ought to be ashamed of yourself!'

Just then I didn't know what she meant.

17

Bob Cuero was still outside. I whistled him up, and we each took one of Miss Fell's arms. She went along between us, her head bent a little.

A couple came out of an apartment across the way, and the woman called: 'Good, evening, Miss Fell.'

Miss Fell had to clear her throat before she answered. She was probably trying to sound cheerful, but it didn't come out that way.

The couple walked towards the parked cars, and we waited. Miss Fell said: 'It's all right. They know I take care of Dave's — Dr. Wagner's — apartment for him when he's away.'

'Good God, Miss Fell, do you think Bob and I care if you're having an affair with a doctor? Or anybody else?'

She didn't answer that. Because of the difference in our heights, I hadn't noticed before, but she was crying. Now she looked up at the night sky and said: 'Oh, I wanted to help so much, and I've just made a mess of things!'

'Help kidnappers?' My hand on her arm tightened. 'Why, a decent woman like you? You're not even in love with one of those cheesewits, if my guess about the doctor's right.'

'Oh, kidnapping. A policeman's technicality. There's justice, and that's a lot bigger than law! But you wouldn't know about that, Lieutenant Bastian.'

She knew my name. I had never heard Bob Cuero use anything but my title, perhaps because of the language difficulty. Something was going on that I didn't know about. I'd been expected in Cedar Ridge, expected by this very zealous do-gooder that I had thought I'd cleverly detected showing guilt.

There was a big question as to who was the hunter and who was the hunted. The answer to the question seemed to be that I was a simple-minded patsy. One man had knocked me down, and when I came to, there was another man there who sympathized with me. So I went with the second man off the highway, out of the world I had known and into this tiny reservation settlement where I could be taken care of with neatness and privacy.

But there was nothing I could do but go forward. For one thing, Bob Cuero had a gun and I didn't; for another, unless and until I recovered Ralph and Miss Beaumont, I was no good to myself or the world. They certainly were not on my backtrack, so — I went forward.

Miss Fell stepped out from between us and knocked on an apartment door. The apartment, as seen from the court where we were, was completely dark; but after she'd rapped a couple of hards and a couple of softs, the knob turned and the door opened.

It was the man who had showed me the badge in Gallup, who'd talked me up the alley. He blinked, said: 'What the hell?' and then, seeing me, went for his waist.

But Bob Cuero had his own gun out, and levelled, and held about two feet away from the man, correctly, as taught in police and judo school. Rule One: Never touch the suspect with the gun, or he can disarm you.

Bob Cuero said: 'Me an' the lieutenant's comin' in. Take his gun, Lieutenant.'

I felt like telling him to stop acting. But
all the elements in this foul-up were
shifting. You couldn't tell the good guys
from the bad guys, and I had forgotten to
buy a program. So I went around the man
in the doorway, jerked him forward out of
the door and got his gun. I felt better with
it. Then we went in, pushing the man and
Miss Fell ahead of us and both of us
— Bob Cuero and I — jumping to one
side as soon as we were through the door.
It was obvious that he'd been educated in
the same sort of MP school I had gone to.
It should have been obvious when he
saluted the captain of Navajo police;
nobody salutes as smartly as an MP.

But nobody took a shot at the open
doorway. I found the light switch and
flipped the lights on quickly, and got away
from the switch just as quickly; but still
nobody took a potshot at me.

The lights disclosed four people: the cheesewit I'd pulled out of the swimming pool at
Cupra, the hard-talking ex-con I'd batted
in the mouth there, their un-charming

lady companion — and Miss Beaumont.

She was on a couch, tied up, and her eyes were closed. I didn't know if she was alive or dead. The whole world fell apart for me, and I wanted to run over and grab her up; I wanted to use my gun on the whole nest of cheesewits, I wanted —

But there was still Ralph to worry about, and I didn't know which side Bob Cuero was really on. I took my time, like it didn't mean much to me, and got over to her and bent down, putting my head on her chest. I heard a heartbeat, and the world started going around again for me.

The cheesewit woman was saying: 'Oh, Dotty, Dotty, that's the cop, oh my God.'

Miss Fell seemed to be named Dotty. She said: 'I couldn't help myself, Myra. Anyway, they can't do anything to you. They have no more jurisdiction here than Harry has.'

Harry was the one whose gun I now held. He said: 'Ha. I got none.'

Miss Fell's prim lips pursed up. 'I thought Myra told me you were a police officer.'

'Special deputy in Las Vegas,' Harry

said. So at least he'd had some right to the buzzer he'd flashed at me.

'Jurisdiction isn't necessary in a felony,' I said. 'Anyone can make a citizen's arrest if he proceeds to turn the arrestee over to the proper authorities with all due diligence. And this is a hell of a time for a lecture on criminal law.'

'I can assure you that I'm not a habitual lawbreaker,' Miss Fell said, completely unnecessarily. 'But when an injustice is being perpetrated, it's anyone's Christian duty to act.'

'Wow!' was about all I could say to that. I looked at them. The one named Harry seemed to have more sense than the ex-con named Morgan or the cheese-wit named Skippy. The woman finished last in the brain derby. I said: 'Harry, you got the boy here?'

Harry nodded. Then his lips moved for a minute, and you could see him make a decision. 'Yeah,' he said. 'And we're worried about him. He don't act right.'

'He's psycho,' I said.

The cheesewit woman, Myra, let out a whoop. 'No, no!'

'Somebody shut her up,' I said, 'or I will.' I hefted the gun barrel as though I was going to slug her with it; something I've never done to a lady. But everything has a first time, and maybe I would have. She shut up, and I said: 'There's his screw-tightener there, knocked out on the couch. What's wrong with her?'

Harry made another of his open face decisions. 'Myra there gave her some sleeping pills. We — made her swallow them.'

Letting them know that Miss Beaumont meant anything to me would be a mistake; if a ruckus started, I didn't want them using her as a hostage. I said: 'Officer Cuero, keep them covered while I look at my boy.' I didn't get between Bob Cuero and any of them as I went for the bedroom door. This apartment was identical with Miss Fell's; they had real democracy at Cedar Ridge.

The bedroom had heavy drapes — a doctor has to sleep in the daytime sometimes — and a big, wooden bedstead. Ralph was on the bed, tied up like Miss Beaumont was, but he wasn't passed out. His eyes were wide and wild-looking, his mouth was gagged, and his skin was pale. When I touched his face to untie the gag, his skin was cold as a fish's.

He didn't yell when I ungagged him. He just stared at me. I said: 'Ralph, Ralph boy, it's Andy. The trouble's over now. I'm here and I've got everything under control.' More or less. There were quite a few unsolved problems.

He still didn't say anything, but he took to shaking. The shivers seemed to start at his ankles and walk up his body; the very strands of his hair almost joined in the act. He didn't seem to know me; he didn't shrink away from me or anything, but he'd lost control completely. I patted his shoulder, not knowing if he felt it or not, and went back into the living room. I said: 'He's very likely to die if somebody doesn't wake up the brain doctor there. This is an M.D.'s apartment, right, Miss Fell?'

The do-gooder nodded, her thin face gray in the electric light.

'Then see if you can dig up some

caffeine or something. If not, make some double-strength coffee, and we'll see if we can feed it to her.'

The doughy-faced Myra was moaning at a nice clip; her Navajo jewelry swung in time to her racket. I went back into the bedroom with Miss Fell and covered her while she looked in the medicine chest. She said: 'Oh, everything here has a fancy name or a prescription number. The doctor would have taken his bag with him.'

'All right, then, the coffee.'

Leaning on the half-wall that divided the kitchenette from the living room proper, I could watch Miss Fell and the rest of them at the same time. She was putting water on to boil, getting out powdered coffee.

Bob Cuero looked at me and then went into the bedroom, his gun still in his hand. I looked at Harry and Morgan and Skippy and said: 'Can't one of you shut that dame up?'

Harry said: 'It would be a great big fat pleasure, but I might kill her.'

Bob Cuero came back. He stood facing

me, but he was careful not to get between me and the cheesewits. He said: 'Lieutenant, you told me that boy didn't beat my girl.'

'That's right, Bob.'

'He's crazy as a mess sergeant. He coulda done anything.'

Miss Fell dropped a spoon on the tile counter of the kitchenette. At that exact moment, the teakettle she'd put on started to whistle. I damn near jumped out of my skin. But I got a grip on myself and said: 'You took my word he hadn't, but I suppose that was to get here. Go back and look at his hands; he couldn't have done a job like that without marking them up.'

'They're all skinned up,' Bob Cuero said, and hefted the gun in his hand. 'No sale, Lieutenant.'

Harry was coming over on my side with everything he said. What he said now was: 'He had a fit. Fell down and had a fit; he was beatin' his hands on the ground. That's why I tied him up.'

'Harry, what are you?' That was me, keeping Bob Cuero's mind off the boy.

'Bouncer in a Las Vegas gambling room?'

'Yeah,' Harry said sadly. 'And I sure wish I was back there.'

Bob Cuero hadn't even listened. He said: 'The scrapes on his hands, sure, they're fresh. But there's no way for me to tell what was on them before he got them scrapes.'

Myra had shifted into passing gear; her whoops and hollers were now shriller, more like shrieks and yelps. I snatched up a pillow from the couch where Miss Beaumont was still tied up, and batted Myra on the head with it.

Cheesewit Skippy came out of his chair. 'That's my dame you're pushing around, copper!'

With the greatest of pleasure, I stiffened my left hand and pushed the tips of my fingers into his solar plexus. He was about as muscular as jail oatmeal. He turned a delicate shade of yellow and sat down again, one hand holding his belly, the other over his mouth.

This had a highly desirable effect. Myra stopped making noises and went over to comfort him.

'True love,' I said. 'Last night she pushed him out into the night, Morgan, in order to pull you into her bed. Tonight she can't bear to see him hurt.'

Morgan said: 'Drop dead, fuzz,' and cut a hard hand through the air derisively.

Bob Cuero was on him fast. He grabbed Morgan's hands, looked at the knuckles, and frowned. Then he reached up the tough guy's sleeves and pulled his ex-white shirt cuffs down. They were both stiff with old blood, and he'd folded them back to hide the stains. Telling me off had unfolded one of them.

Officer Bob Cuero shifted the gun to his left hand and hit Morgan's chin as hard as he could with his right fist. Morgan went over backward, chair and all, and lay still. Bob Cuero rolled him over and pulled a heavy pair of leather gloves out of his hip pocket. They were stiff with something.

Miss Fell said: 'I've got the coffee ready.' So I backed up and worked my pocket knife out and slashed Miss Beaumont's bonds. I should have done it before, but too much was going on, and I hadn't wanted to call too much attention to her.

Bob Cuero stood there, looking down at Morgan. I said: 'You could kick him to death, Bob. I'd testify he got it resisting arrest, and any testimony these cheesewits gave wouldn't be listened to.'

The patrolman looked at me. There was still no expression on his face, but his eyes were shiny; he could cry all right. 'I was gonna,' he said. 'I was gonna catch him an' let him have it, but goddamit, I'm a policeman. I better take him over to them Navajo cops and turn him in.'

He took handcuffs off his hip and bent down, hauled Morgan to his feet, and cuffed him, unconscious as he was. 'I'll wait till he can walk. Think any of the others was in on it, Lieutenant?' He let the manacled man fall to the floor again.

'No.' I thought I was telling the truth for once. Skippy was too soft, Myra not the type — she'd have been screaming all over the Cupra night — and Harry hadn't joined them till today. 'Can you leave all this mess out of your story, Bob? You do and I'm sure Morgan will; felonious

265

assault's enough without kidnapping.'

'Why should I? Why, Lieutenant?'

'There's a boy in there, no older than your daughter. Give him a good hard police grilling, haul him into court, and he may be off his rocker for life.'

Myra opened her mouth again. 'You can't — ' I batted her with the pillow, she shut up, and I watched Bob Cuero.

'They're gonna ask me how I got up here.'

'I drove you,' I said. 'I'm an old army buddy, and I drove you.'

He turned this over. I gave him time, and watched Miss Fell holding Miss Beaumont's head up, spooning the thick coffee between her lips. Some color was coming back into Miss Beaumont's face; she was going to make it. I hoped she'd know something to do for Ralph when she did come to.

Bob Cuero suddenly grinned. 'I thought we was in the same outfit in the army,' he said. He mentioned a number, and I nodded; an MP company I'd commanded. 'I was right,' Bob Cuero said. 'But I never did get your last name.'

'Your prisoner's stirring,' I said. 'Funny I don't remember you.'

'You got your gold leaves an' transferred to staff when I'd been there a week,' Bob Cuero said. He hauled Morgan to his feet, slapped his face, and started pushing him out.

'Hold on, Bob. Who's got the keys to the gray Chevy?'

Harry pulled them out of his pants pocket carefully, making no false moves. I nodded, and he tossed them to Bob Cuero, who caught them and shoved Morgan along again. As he got to the door, Bob Cuero said: 'I made sergeant after you left; it was a good outfit,' and then he was gone.

Miss Beaumont's eyes were opening. So were mine, in a different way; one by one I was getting rid of the crud, and there was still a chance I could get Ralph to Kansas with the privacy that Mr. Bartlett had paid for. I would have earned the money; nobody's ever done more, for any sum at all.

'Harry, think you can walk to Las Vegas?'

The special cop — all bouncers in Vegas are specials, it doesn't mean a thing — blinked at me. A little smile played around his tight mouth. 'Pushing a peanut with my nose, mister. On my hands and knees.'

Miss Fell said: 'Take the Thoreau road. There'll be Navajo pickups going down the highway.'

Harry stood up. He was watching me as though he didn't believe his good luck. 'I promise, Lieutenant, you don't have to worry about blackmail, not from me.'

'Thanks for nothing, pal. You couldn't try it without confessing to kidnapping.'

He stopped his shuffle towards freedom. 'It wasn't, though. He come of his own accord, the kid did. He *wanted* to come. So help me.'

I shook my head. I was no screw-tightener, no headshrinker. There was no way I could judge what a boy in Ralph's condition would do. I said: 'So if he did, you still kidnapped Miss Beaumont there.'

She said: 'No. I went along to try and protect Ralph. I knew you'd catch up with us, Andy.'

'Couldn't you have stopped him? I

mean, you're in the business of straightening bent brains.'

Her eyes were still dreamy, but she was holding her own coffee cup now. Maybe barking at her would bring her around; with Bob Cuero gone, I needed her.

She snapped: 'Don't you yell at me! Oh, Andy, he was so miserable — Ralph was — and he thought maybe nobody wanted him, his father was just shoving him off — and he wanted to try something new.'

'Welcome to the land of the living. I won't yell at you again. Ralph's just crazy, he isn't stupid. I can't imagine him wanting to try life and love among the cheesewits . . . When you get that coffee down, go in and see him. I think he's in bad shape.'

She looked at me curiously. 'You're so smart about some things, Andy, and so slow about others.' She tilted the cup, wiped her mouth inelegantly on the back of her hand, and got up, straightening her skirt into place.

But this wasn't the time to dwell on the beauties and allure of Miss Beaumont. I barked 'Next,' like a barber shaving pigs in the slaughterhouse, and turned on Miss Fell. 'You, pal. You're no cheesewit, and God knows you're not the typical criminal — for which my whole trade gives thanks. What are you doing in this lash-up?'

She sat straight on the couch; I'm sure that at some school or other she had been made to carry books on her head. She said: 'Myra is a friend of mine. She used to teach arts and crafts in the Indian school, before they closed it. And I don't like people like you, Lieutenant, who push people around for a living.'

'Fair enough,' I said. 'But that's a pretty big not liking, to get yourself involved as an accessory to an assault and a kidnapping.'

This was one you couldn't intimidate. 'I knew nothing of any assault, and I do not consider it kidnapping to restore a boy to his own mother.'

And then, finally, I got it. Nobody ever said I was bright; just big, hard-working and well-trained. But finally I got it.

Myra, of course, was Ralph's mother.

18

I went over, patted Skippy for guns, and hefted Myra's handbag. No arms, no armour. I heaved my own gun up in the air, caught it and put it in my holster, where it fit very well; it should have, since it was the one Harry had taken away from me in Gallup.

Then I sat down. I was a police officer without police business. No crime had been committed, except the brutal one of the assault on the Cuero girl, and Bob Cuero was out in the night taking care of that. He'd do it well, too; my sergeants had trained him.

Neither Ralph nor Miss Beaumont had been kidnapped. They'd gone with the cheesewits of their own free will; Ralph because Myra was his mother, Miss Beaumont because she wouldn't leave Ralph.

Of course, Ralph had a normal guy's reaction to finding out Myra was his mother — he'd gone out of his head. Looking back, hell, every time he'd had a bad fit, he'd seen her: once — in the inspection station — before I had, and once in the night, standing in a skimpy, sleazy piece of underwear against the motel lights. First time, he'd bawled out an agricultural inspector. Second time, he'd fainted.

And then, something else rolled into my head. He'd fainted another time, too. Outside the party, in Cupra . . .

I said: 'Miss Beaumont, Ralph ever faint when you were taking care of him in his house?'

'Why, no. Once, before I went on the case, the doctor said, but — '

So his mother had been with Morgan when the rat beat up the Indian woman. He had seen his mother. He never fainted unless he did . . . He'd been nervous for God knew how long — years, maybe — but until Myra and Skippy came up to him back in Naranjo Vista, he hadn't taken to fainting; hadn't really gotten crazy enough for his father to risk publicity by sending him away for treatment.

There was no doubt about it Myra was an accessory, even an accomplice, to the beating of Peggy Sue Cuero. It was my duty — my manifest duty, one of the lecturers at MP school used to call it — to turn her over to Bob Cuero.

And I wasn't going to do it.

Not — I hoped — because of Mr. Bartlett's money, and the privacy he'd paid me for, which would be completely wiped out if his wife was pinched. But because of Ralph. Dropping, fainting Ralph.

He was maybe nuts, but he was a sensitive kind of nuts. Sooner or later he would get to thinking that he'd helped send his own mother over, and then — I didn't have to be a screw-tightener to figure it out — he would go past the point where a cure was possible.

I wasn't going to do that to him. His father'd frozen him till he was half-crazy, and his mother'd shoved him over the line. He thought of me as his friend, and I wasn't going to turn on him for all the money, all the badges and oaths of office, in the world. Call him loony. At least he was trying.

But back to my muttons, as the French are supposed to say. What crimes did I have left on my hands? Oh, I'd been socked on the head by Harry down in Gallup, but I wasn't anxious to get publicity on that.

Miss Beaumont had been standing, watching me. She took a deep breath and raised her good chin. She said: 'I'll go see what I can do about Ralph. Maybe I can talk him back to some sense.'

Myra said: 'He's just as sensible as anyone else. But people can't live without love, and his father doesn't know how to love anyone or anything but success. He's just a great big success story, that's what Sidney Bartlett is..'

Skippy said: 'That's right, love is the most important thing in the world.' He put out his fat hand and took Myra's knucklesful of rings in it.

'Very touching,' I said. 'Isn't it, Miss Fell? Two lonesome souls, wandering around the world, looking for someone else to blame because they're both messes. Do you agree, Miss Fell?'

She said clearly: 'I think you're one of

the most hateful men I've ever met in my entire life. Don't you have any compassion at all?'

'Not for cheesewits, Miss Fell.'

She snorted. I sat there, thinking hard. My eyes burned from fatigue. I felt like I'd smoked a carton of cigarettes since dawn, and dawn was a long ways back. It was like having a hangover without the memory of a good time.

'All right,' I said. I was just stalling, looking forward to the moment when Miss Beaumont reported. She wasn't likely to come out and say that Ralph was hopeless, pushed to the point where he was incurable, because she wouldn't have that much faith in her professional judgment; but I did. Even if she hadn't gotten her doctor's degree yet, I believed that what she couldn't do, no one in her trade could. It was a curious conclusion for me to reach; the first time in my life I'd ever had complete faith in anyone.

'All right,' I said again. 'Let's go over it. Skippy, you and Myra were up in Las Vegas. Morgan'd be a capper for a gambling place, a guy whose job it is to get rich suckers in. You, Myra, you'd have money. Mr. Bartlett would see that you got a decent alimony. Right?'

Myra said: 'Yes, but I don't see how you figured it out, and — '

'You were going to pay Morgan to get Ralph for you. For your own damned sentimental reasons, or maybe because if you had Ralph, Mr. Bartlett could be made to pay you more.'

'I love him!' she wailed. 'I'm his mother!'

'Sure. A one-hundred-percent American mother, living with this slob here, cheating on him with that craps hustler Morgan. You went to see Ralph a few days ago, and it toppled him into a nervous breakdown, didn't it? He thought you were dead, and then you showed up. And showed up is what I mean; showed yourself up for a sloppy bag.'

Miss Fell said: 'I didn't know the human race contained people like you.'

'I'm not running a popularity contest,' I said. 'I'm trying to figure something out. If this piece of female flesh could give birth to a boy like Ralph, the human race isn't lost, Miss Fell. That's a ray of cheer for a do-gooder like you.'

'Thank you very much.'

Myra was giving out one of her moaning screeches again. 'Don't let him talk to me like that, Skippy. Make him stop it.'

'How?' I asked. None of them bothered to answer that, especially Skippy. 'So you called up Morgan in Vegas, and he came to help you. Morgan and Skippy here cased us when we were leaving Mr. Bartlett's house.'

Myra said: 'How would you feel if they were taking your boy to the sanitarium? Your own son?'

'Considering that you were the one who tipped him over, the question doesn't get an answer. He was all right till you showed up, wasn't he? What did you do, walk up to him on the street with your arms held out?'

Skippy cut in. 'He wouldn't come with us. Me, I didn't care. Who wants a kid trailing along? But you buy the cow, you get the calf.'

'Beautifully put,' I said. 'Even if it doesn't mean anything. Miss Fell, did you know the human race contained people like these two? And Morgan, who tried to put the snatch on Ralph in Cupra, and when an Indian girl interfered, beat her up? Did you know about people like that, Miss Fell?'

Her thin face was pale in the doctor's lamplight. She said: 'I don't see why you're so intent on making a good impression on me.'

'How would you like it, being a tough cop in a world that has learned there's nothing so loathsome as a tough cop? But the work has to be done. You can see that right here, right now. By me, and guys like Bob Cuero. The one he took out of here, we get them all the time. The girl, Cuero's daughter, she probably just spoke up to him and told him to leave Ralph alone. So he socked her, and it felt so good to him, he went on socking her till she's in the hospital. There have to be guys like us to take care of guys like him, Miss Fell.'

'You're human, after all,' she said. 'You care whether people like you?'

'Who the hell made this generation of Americans into a generation of police haters . . . ?' I laughed, though I didn't feel like it. 'I sound like the cheesewits here, wanting to be loved. Okay, Skippy. Morgan made his play at the party in Cupra. I'm assuming he didn't tell you that in the course of his try, he beat up a girl. I'm assuming it because if I assumed anything else, I'd have to turn you over to Bob Cuero as accessories.'

'Morgan didn't tell us. I swear. He just said it was too rough, and he wanted out, and he was going to send for a friend, a real strong man. That was Harry. He met up with us this morning,' Skippy said. 'He took you off in Gallup. A very hard guy.' Skippy rubbed his soft hands over his soft face, and shivered. 'Lieutenant, I was just trying to make Myra happy. If you'd let us go . . . '

'That depends on what Ralph wants. If Ralph — '

Miss Beaumont was back. For all her youth, she looked dead tired; she had a right to be. She said: 'Andy, Ralph wants to talk to you.'

'By God, you're a miracle worker, Miss Beaumont.'

279

'Olga,' she said. 'Why, all I did was untie him and show some confidence.'

I went into the bedroom. I don't know what I'd expected to see, but it wasn't anything bad. Ralph was sitting in a deep chair under a reading lamp. I guess the doc got up sometimes at night and smoked a cigarette there, maybe studied. I sat down on the edge of the bed.

Ralph's eyes were rolling, his mouth opening and closing like he'd just run the four-minute mile. I said: 'What are you scared about now, Ralph?'

'I — I ran away.'

What did he expect me to do, whip out a blackjack and sock him? 'We all do, kid. And she's your mother.'

He shuddered, making one of his mental stands. 'Yes. Yes, the mother-search is stressed by every modern psychologist as an important personality component, and cannot — '

'Shut up!'

He gulped and, to my surprise, shut up. He even said: 'Yes, Andy.'

'You could have been killed. You could have gotten Miss Beaumont killed.'

His long fingers went up through his hair. 'You're attracted to her, aren't you? Are you in love with her, Andy?' This was normal boyish curiosity.

'You got us all into a fine mess, boy.'

He said: 'Yes, you are in love with her. Changing the subject is a very typical sign. I'm making a study of analysis by conversation, character ana — Andy! Let's get out of here! Let's get on to the booby hatch.' That doubled him up with the pain he felt and sent his head down to his knees, his hands hugging himself.

The time had come to use the MP bark. So I barked: 'Break it off!'

He was a sick boy. People had cajoled him, put ice packs on his head, reasoned with him. They hadn't bawled him out. Surprise snapped his head up and made his eyes hold still as he stared at me.

I went to the door, just keeping myself from using the bark on Miss Beaumont. My voice was real genteel as I said her name. She stood up and came towards the bedroom door. I held it for her, and took time to look over the cheesewits. Miss Fell looked sick, and Myra and Skippy looked like cheesewits who needed a drink.

Then I shut the bedroom door, and looked from Miss Beaumont to Ralph. I said: 'Lady, the time has come to level with us. Forget you haven't hung out your doctor's sign yet, and give us the cold dope. How nuts is Ralph?'

She said: 'That word doesn't mean anything. Ralph is disturbed; he needs treatment. There's been no injury to his brain.'

'That doesn't mean a damned thing. If you'd read three books more and gotten a license to be a screw-tightener — '

'Clinical psychologist,' she said.

'You sound like Miss Fell out there. If you were a clinical psychologist, would you send Ralph over? Send him to the mental clinic, is what I mean, of course.'

She stood there straight inside the bedroom door, as good a soldier as Bob Cuero. Then she said: 'He'll need protracted therapy, consultations, but his insight is very good. He should respond beautifully to treatment.' She took a deep breath. 'Historically speaking, he's had a light neurosis — not crippling — for some years. Probably since the onset of puberty. It deepened, became completely inhibiting a short time ago, when he received a severe shock. The grooves of the crippling neurosis are not yet deep; those of the previous, protracted one may never be erased. But most of us have to go through life with some neurotic failings.'

'A beautiful report, Miss Beaumont. Don't you think so, Ralph?'

He tried to grin. 'She — she never wasted a word, Andy.'

'Okay, Miss Beaumont. G'wan and keep the cheesewits company.'

She said: 'I do think you could call me Olga, Andy,' but she went.

I said: 'This is the time to pull up your socks, kid. No going off screaming. Look, pal. I was an orphanage kid. Every damn brat in the home used to have the same dream; that it was a mistake, that we had a mama. Mine was tall and cool and she'd always just had a bath.'

He took a deep shuddering breath. 'You used to have that dream, Andy?'

'Yeah. And if that slob out there had shown up and said she was my mother, maybe I'd have gone off my rocker, too.

Maybe I'd have been a candidate for the booby hatch.'

He ran his hands down the thighs of his trousers, then through his hair. He grinned a little. 'Don't call it that, Andy.'

'All right. Mental hospital, sanitarium, clinic. The staff there are very fine people.'

He had grown up. He said: 'Very fine people for some cases. Not for mine. I'm completely rejected. My father was going to send me to the booby — to the sanitarium sooner than give me up to my mother. He lied to me all my life to keep anyone from knowing he'd made a mistake and married the wrong woman. My mother doesn't love me. How could she, and love someone like Skippy at the same time?'

'That's a lot of questions,' I said. 'Tell you the truth, I don't know the answer, a dumb cop like me. But you will, when you grow up. With that brain of yours, you'll know the answer to a lot of things I'll never know. What do you want to do?'

He stood up and walked up and down in front of the chair; two steps, then back, then two steps. There wasn't a hell of a lot of room to move around in. He said finally: 'What can I do? I don't want to go back to my father, I don't want to live with my mother. I went out of my head when I saw what she was. She was even a little drunk when she spoke to me.'

'Weak people take a drink before they do anything. Where did she speak to you?'

'Outside the library. I've been having special tutors, but they let me go to the library alone. Skippy was with her, both drunk.'

'Both weak people,' I repeated my little gem of knowledge.

'Weak people?' he asked. 'You mean cheesewits, don't you?' Then he started laughing, I guess at my face. 'Andy, I've no place to go except where my father wanted me to go. Believe me, it won't be so bad. I'll be learning about the inside of a mental clinic, and so long as I'm learning something interesting, I'm kind of happy. I've known that since I was seven or eight years old.' He came over and put a hand on my shoulder. 'Don't worry. It's only four or five years till I'm of age. Five years and a month,' he said.

'I'll write to you, Andy.'

'If they let you. I don't know. Maybe they'll put you to making wicker baskets and take your books away.'

He shook his head. 'It's not your grief,' he said. 'It's mine. I've given up kicking and screaming when things don't go the way I want them. I've grown up. I could have gotten you killed, I could have gotten your woman killed and thrown out on a Navajo road. Miss Beaumont, I mean. Cheesewits who'd crack a tie rod to slow people down would do anything. This is what they call the checkerboard area, Andy. Very badly patrolled, since title to the land and the jurisdiction thereof rests in several directions — county, federal . . . '

'No legal lectures just now, kid.'

He laughed. 'I'm a bore sometimes, I guess. I put you and Miss Beaumont in danger. Harry had a gun; it's in the glove compartment now.'

'He had two. The other one he took away from me. I'm not much of a cop, Ralph.'

He started to go under again. 'Let's get going! I don't like it here, it smells of

— of her. Let's — ' He broke it off with a long painful breath, then rubbed his face. 'I'm all right now. I've got to learn not to give in to those things. Maybe I can control it if I try.'

'Go in the bathroom and use some cold water on your face. There's no way out of here except past Myra — your mother, kid — so you'll have to see her again. You're no damned genie that can go into smoke and sneak out through a keyhole.'

In the bathroom, he turned. 'You say you're dumb, Andy, but you're not.'

'Thanks a million, Ralph.'

He came out with one of his unsuccessful hairdos and grabbed my forearm in his bony fingers. 'I'm glad I have a friend, Andy.'

'What I've been trying to tell you.'

'I know.'

We went out into the living room together. I said: 'Miss Beaumont, let's roll. Miss Fell, I leave these cheesewits to you. I doubt if they'll walk away, so long as the food holds out. Explain them to your doctor pal when he gets back.'

She said: 'Cedar Ridge will improve the

minute your car starts.'

'Thank you.' I started for the door. Then I stopped. While I had the bat in my hand, I might as well take one more crack at the ball. 'I could send you over,' I said. 'All three of you. For cracking the tie rod on the Cadillac. Don't forget that.'

Skippy said: 'Morgan said the car wouldn't start at all. I didn't know.'

The top of my head blew off. I haven't lost my temper often enough in my adult life to get used to it. 'Didn't know,' I yelled. 'Of course you didn't know. Attempted murder, and you didn't know! Listen: in Paris, after the war, there was the toughest gang I ever heard of. They used to steal drugs from American medical installations.'

Skippy brightened: 'M?' he asked. 'H?'

Myra said: 'Hush, lover.'

'Yeah,' I said. 'Hush, lover. They used to steal penicillin. The way they did it was this: one of them would cut himself, and be found bleeding on a sentry's beat. When the sentry bent over to see what it was, another'd jump on his back and strangle him; garrote, the French call it.

Then they'd heist the drugs and throw a firebomb into a hospital ward to cover their getaway.'

'What a fascinating life you've led,' Miss Fell said.

Miss Beaumont and Ralph were staring at me; the cheesewits were just staring.

'All right,' I said. 'Well. I'd rather go up against five of that gang, and me single-handed, than two cheesewits trying to be loved on Saturday night, with 'I didn't do it' on the tips of their tongues and 'I didn't mean to do it,' in the backs of their throats. Morgan told you that cracking the tie rod wouldn't kill anybody! Didn't you ever try thinking for yourselves?'

Myra started to cry. Skippy was just blinking, like a kid whose teacher has made him stand in the corner. After all, his mush-head was probably saying, 'I didn't throw the first spitball.'

Miss Beaumont had stood up and moved nearer Ralph, protecting a flank that no longer needed protecting.

Myra let out one of her jewelry-bouncing screeches, my lecture forgotten. 'When will I see you again, Ralphie?'

He turned, and you could see the man he was going to be in a few years. He said: 'Probably never, Mother.'

This upped her decibels a few notches, but Skippy reached out and took her arm. 'Kid's right, Myra.'

She collapsed into Skippy's arms, and that was the last we saw of them. We got into our battered Cadillac with the right-hand inside door handle missing, and I turned the radiator towards 66, and the road to Kansas.

Miss Beaumont sat very straight between us. But I don't need two hands to drive a good car on a dry road; I dropped the right one over hers, where they were neatly folded in her tailored lap. She looked surprised more than anything; she didn't know that little things like this weren't going to bother Ralph anymore.

On her other side, Ralph was crying, but gently, just tears rolling down the face he turned away from us. I'd have done a lot worse than cry if my orphan-dreams had turned into his kind of reality when I was his age.

When he blew his nose, we were five

miles out of Cedar Ridge, five miles nearer old 66. I said: 'Make them let you write to me from the Nutcracker Suite, Ralph. And I'll write to you. Now and then the department gets a case you could help me on.'

'All right,' he said. 'There are sure to be books on criminology in the clinic hospital.'

'When you get out,' I said, 'maybe you can come live with me. There's an extra bedroom in my flat.'

'Hey, that'd be a winging hoedown!'

Miss Beaumont wriggled her fingers out from under mine. 'How about me?' she asked.

I guess she meant to ask if Ralph wanted her to write to him, too, but I said: 'Aw, you can come live with us, too. But you'll have to marry one of us. Ralph's ten years younger than you are. I'm twelve years older. Take your choice.'

She gasped, and Ralph started to laugh. It ended with a wild neurotic honk, but for a few minutes he held it; just loud laughter, like any kid his age would laugh.

GHOST LAKE

V. J. Banis

Its real name is Caspar Lake, but people call it Ghost Lake. Years ago, a ferryboat went down in a storm, drowning everyone on board — and some say their souls have never rested . . . Beth Nolan travels to the nearby town at the invitation of an old school friend, but no sooner does she arrive than she is plunged into the murky depths of the brutal murder of a young woman. Beth must find answers — or risk joining the dead in the haunted depths of Ghost Lake . . .

THE EYE STONES

Harriet Esmond

A shock awaits Deborah Ritchie when she arrives to stay with her recently married sister. She is told that the couple have both perished tragically in a fire which destroyed their home. Alone in the bleak Norfolk brecklands, Deborah is forced to accept hospitality from the forbidding Sir Randall Gaunt. She gladly leaves Sir Randall and his grim anatomical practices for the warm companionship of young Lord Stannard and his family. But before long, she is inextricably involved in a nightmare of mystery and unimagined evil . . .

ANCIENT EVIL RETURNS
& Other Stories

Richard A. Lupoff

A youthful journalist seeks to unravel the mysterious disaster that struck a New England town nearly a century ago . . . A young couple, stranded by a monstrous storm, seek shelter in a darkened town and discover a dangerous cult . . . A peculiar child is born . . . A young woman and her boyfriend find themselves in terrible danger . . . A brilliant academic begins to make a disquieting discovery . . . These are the problems faced by ordinary people as they encounter extraordinary mysteries when *Ancient Evil Returns*.

COLD CALLING
& Other Stories

Geraldine Ryan

Pronounced unfit for frontline duty due to injury, and eligible to retire in a year, DS Fran Phoenix is given a new job heading up the cold cases team — or 'put in a corner' in the basement, as she sees it. Teamed up with a PC with barely two years' experience, they reopen the twenty-five-year-old case of a missing girl — but evidence continues to be thin on the ground. Can the oddly matched duo heat up the trail and uncover the truth? Three stories from the pen of Geraldine Ryan.

LORD JAMES HARRINGTON AND THE CORNISH MYSTERY

Lynn Florkiewicz

While on holiday with his wife Beth in Cornwall, James learns that a local fisherman vanished during the recent opening procession of the Cornish Legends Festival. When more men disappear in broad daylight, he can't help but put his sleuthing hat on. If they were kidnapped, why is there no ransom demand? What are the flashing lights off the coastline? Who is the eccentric woman on the moors? Have the Cornish Legends really come to life? As James delves into the mystery, he realizes his questions come at a price . . .

REDEMPTION TRAIL

Victor Rosseau

Petty criminal Alfred Collins finds himself the victim of a conspiracy to frame him for murder. Sentenced to twenty years in prison, he manages to effect a daring escape, and assumes a new identity. Eventually he learns that the man who framed him has fled to work for a lumbering company. Consumed with the passion for revenge and the thought of being able to force a confession that would clear his name and free him from the life of a fugitive, Collins follows his trail into the Canadian wilderness . . .